ETNA

ETNA

PAUL YOON

SCRIBNER
EDITIONS

London · New York · Amsterdam/Antwerp · Sydney/Melbourne · Toronto · New Delhi

First published in the United States by Scribner, an imprint of Simon & Schuster LLC, 2026
First published in Great Britain by Scribner Editions, an imprint of Simon & Schuster UK Ltd, 2026

1 3 5 7 9 10 8 6 4 2

Simon & Schuster UK Ltd, 7th Floor, 199 Bishopsgate,
London, EC2M 3TY

Simon & Schuster Australia, Sydney

Simon & Schuster India, New Delhi

www.simonandschuster.co.uk
www.simonandschuster.com.au
www.simonandschuster.co.in

The authorised representative in the EEA is Simon & Schuster Netherlands BV, Herculesplein 96, 3584 AA Utrecht, Netherlands. info@simonandschuster.nl

A CIP catalogue record for this book is available from the British Library

Trade Paperback ISBN: 978-1-3985-5920-2
eBook ISBN: 978-1-3985-5921-9
Audio: 978-1-3985-5922-6

Printed and Bound in the UK using 100% Renewable Electricity at CPI Group (UK) Ltd

FSC www.fsc.org
MIX
Paper | Supporting responsible forestry
FSC® C013604

For Bill Clegg and Marysue Rucci

For Oscar

. . . In the end, you do what the voice tells you.
It says forget, you forget.
It says begin again, you begin again.

—LOUISE GLÜCK

Blood finds no sea.

—J. M. LEDGARD

THE FIELD

Look! See the dogs . . .

I was born near water.

I was born on a farm where many other dogs and other animals were born and cared for and lived.

I would never learn what the farm was intending to do with me. Maybe nothing at all. Maybe I was supposed to grow old there.

Or maybe I was always supposed to leave. To go work somewhere else and be with a new family.

But it was home to me. My mother was there. My brothers and my sisters. An early memory: waking up to a den of pale noses surrounding me before our mother came, the silhouette of her face looming over us in the sky, the tall triangles of her ears pocketing the smell of the coast.

Every day there was sand floating in daylight and the salt on our tongues. The sea wind over grass. The barn eaves where hornets made nests that resembled the empty shells of turtles hanging up there heavy in the wind.

The cloven hooves of goats and the enormous sleepy pig who never wanted to play with us.

And the birds. Birds everywhere. Their bright feathers and their music. Their shadows and all their shit, which I loved to eat.

I loved, too, listening to the farm owners talking to each other. I liked the softness of their two voices. The woman often speaking through strands of her hair. The way the man rubbed his finger over a button on his shirt when he was preoccupied or nervous. The way they both said *weather* and *child* and *bucket* and *feed* and *bed* and *leak in the roof* and *don't forget about the dogs* and *beautiful* and *happy birthday* and *see you soon, I love you.*

Then there was a day when their voices changed. It reminded me of when the man told the woman that his father had died. There was more silence and space between them, and when they spoke, it was about people fighting along a far border.

As the days went on, the farm owners kept talking about it. Whispering outside as they went to fill our water bowls, to feed the animals. About the country next to this one and then about other countries coming here, too, to help, to fight.

And then one day, not long after, a young woman arrived. She was alone and driving a pickup truck. When she got out, we saw that she was in a uniform. She took off her hat, revealing the long braid of her hair down her back as she approached the couple and said that she was hoping to find dogs to join up with and assist the armies arriving from North America and Europe.

I pretended not to notice her. I stayed close to my mother, who stood tall in the grass, our ears following the humans. I held the sounds of the words *join up* and *armies* and *North America* and *Europe.* I listened to the fabric of the young woman's uniform moving across her thighs as she walked around, the leafy smell of the back of her neck suddenly everywhere in the air, pushing away the floating particles of sand.

The pig sleeping. My mother's ears going stiff, and then her heart beating faster. The air inside that empty turtle shell above me vibrating as three shadows rushed across the grass. The woman scooped me up, and suddenly I was in the air and leaving, my mother barking and following until she couldn't follow us anymore.

Later, as we were speeding down a country road, the woman would say that she chose me because she could tell I would grow to be very fast and strong. I was sitting with her up in the front. A rifle was leaning upright between us, and she reached over as she drove and ran her hand down my front leg to my paw, which I did not like.

To my surprise, she apologized—the couple on the farm had never apologized when they touched my paws—and then the woman smiled and explained that she also chose me because we could speak to each other, which wasn't always the case with every dog she met.

It meant that I was special. And that she was in search of dogs that were special.

I didn't understand any of this. I was scared. I whimpered; I wanted to go back. I didn't know where we were going and I had never been in a vehicle before. Everything shook. I was trying not to listen to the scream of the engine and the tires spitting gravel and deep inside me the echo of my mother in the field, stuck behind the fence, and I was trying not to stare at the other dog in the seat behind me, asleep on her belly, paws out, eyes tightly and uncomfortably shut.

The dog was around my age, ten or eleven months, and she carried a faraway smell on her coat that I couldn't locate. Still, even though I had never seen her before today, her smell comforted me. It comforted me because I could no longer smell my mother and my brothers and sisters. My nose had emptied itself of them.

So I clung to the smell of the new dog behind me as the truck kept speeding and shaking and the trees appeared to fly by faster, like they were enormous kites, and the power line whipped up and down like a sea wave.

I licked the rifle barrel, but it tasted bad.

The woman smiled again. What's your name? she said.

Why should I tell you? I quickly said back.

Fair enough, she said. It doesn't matter. You're going to get a new one. A better one.

And then it happened. I stood up straighter and turned toward her, understanding in that moment that she hadn't actually spoken out loud this time, that we were literally communicating with each other in a different way.

With other animals, the common language we were able to form between us, no matter the animal, was also always a silent one. Whenever we communicated, it was like dark shapes appeared and lived in a space between our eyes, shapes we could translate.

With this young woman, it was similar, but I felt her words more physically, and around me: it was like the air was pressing against my ears, and then a small door opened in my head into a corner I had never been inside before. The colors of the day got a little brighter, but less sharp, and it was as though her words, clear, were carried by those bright colors—like the words were currents, vibrating, and I was responding.

I faced the window again and went silent. I tried to focus on the power line outside, but my head now hurt.

It doesn't last, she said, placing a hand on my head. Besides, you'll get used to it. You'll get used to all of this, my darling.

She then told me her own name: Soojin. She was in her late twenties, still young for a human, I knew even then. I focused on the dog's smell behind me—different grass, vomit, clay, forest trees—as Soojin told me she was a doctor: a doctor now in this country's army, but that the Americans had hired her temporarily because they had heard she was good with handling dogs.

They don't know the half of it, she said, and tapped the side of her head and winked.

She said that she doubted I would meet another like her in my life. She had never met or heard about anyone else who could speak to dogs the way she could. She couldn't explain why it was not with every dog, only some of them. Or why it wasn't all animals. What it was about dogs.

She wondered how I felt about all this: whether she was scaring me or delighting me, whether I wanted to say something, anything, back to her right now.

I wanted to say something back, but I also didn't. I could tell she was testing me in some way, but I wasn't sure what the test was. I caught the silhouette of a bird in the air above the trees and I thought again about my mother and my brothers and sisters, and I thought about the couple on the farm and their soft voices even as they worried about the fighting along the border, and I focused again on the smell and the heartbeats of the dog behind me, and then the woman tapped the steering wheel and said it was hard to keep up with my mind.

She pointed her thumb behind us and told me not to worry. The dog had been nauseous from the moving truck—they had been on the road for days—but that she would be fine. She was from a fishing village Soojin had visited, much farther away. The dog was strong, like me.

I named her Fuji, she said.

Fuji?

Her war name, Soojin said. You're all getting war names. You're now war dogs, my darling. You're getting a new home and you'll make new friends and you're going to work hard and save a lot of lives. But we don't have much time. So we have to hurry.

I didn't want a new home. I wanted to go back to the farm. I began to pant.

I knew she could hear me thinking all this, but Soojin just turned a dial in the truck. Cold air hit my neck as she reached across to scratch my chest, which, with the cold air, suddenly felt good.

Briefly, everything vanished except the goodness of that feeling, the cold air, and her scratching. I tried to focus on that.

And then, as she accelerated, passing a line of trucks the same color as her uniform, she named me Etna.

Etna, she said again, letting it settle in her mouth and in the air between us.

Behind the window of one of the trucks, a young man waved. I lost track of the bird.

I repeated my name, *Etna,* as Soojin explained to me what a volcano was and that the one I was named for was on an island called Sicily. She said she had been reading a travel book on Sicily that she had checked out of a library. She realized this morning that she would be very late in returning it.

Soojin scratched my chest one more time.

Did you know, Etna, that there were once hermits in Sicily? she said.

She had told me that it was hard to follow my thoughts, but now I couldn't follow hers: What was she talking about? The woman on the farm sometimes told her husband that he was in his *own world*. Soojin was in her own world, too.

I turned to check on Fuji, who was stirring but had yet to open her eyes. She had rolled to her side; I could now see that she had a pale stripe of fur across her chest.

Soojin kept talking about hermits and cottages on the hillside outside a place called Palermo. She said that in the next life, she'd like to be a hermit. To be alone. To see no one. To be in that tremendous quiet. Or maybe be a hermit with some dogs.

Tell me, Etna, is one a hermit if they have dogs?

I watched cars appear. Many, many of them in the other lane with big bags and small pieces of furniture strapped to the tops, all of them heading in the opposite direction, toward the sea. I tried to smell the sea as a tiny hand reached out and waved. All the sky reflected in the windshields.

Soojin hadn't stopped talking.

Like you, Etna, she said. How about it? Come be a hermit with me one day. And how about Fuji, too?

Fuji stirred again; Soojin glanced up at the small mirror above her. I looked back and my eyes met Fuji's for the first time, and we stayed that way, fixed on each other as Soojin continued to speak:

That's right, my darling, are you feeling better? We're talking about you. Meet Etna. He's strong, like you. Two strong dogs. The pair of you will live in my very own hermit kingdom. So, promise me this: survive. Both of you. Look out for each other. And when this is over, come find me. We'll go to Sicily together.

She took out her phone. She lifted it to her mouth and recorded my new name, that I was a twelve-month-old mixed-breed shepherd, sixty-seven pounds. That I had some sensitivity when my legs and paws were handled, which they would have to work on. And then she commanded the phone to send the message as she drove farther inland, my head hurting less as I pushed my ears forward, catching the bursts of faraway jets.

I thought Fuji and I would be with her from then on. Instead, after driving and driving for hours, past more fields and power lines, Soojin dropped us off at a gas station parking lot, where there were even more trucks and more people in uniforms. More new, loud sounds. We squirmed and kicked and whimpered as she lifted each of us out of the truck and told us that it was going to be difficult but that we had each other now. That we would have to look out for each other and to never forget that we were strong.

She crouched, burying her face into our scruffs, and Fuji and I kept whimpering, unsure about what would happen next, not wanting to part with her, pushing our snouts against her. Then, as we focused on a spot under her chin for the last time—pollen, a pulsing vein, a stranger's lips—Soojin reminded us to remember our promise before she handed us over to a group of uniformed men and left.

During those war years, I would only cross paths with Soojin one more time after that day. It was when I was lying on a cold metal table in a field hospital as a doctor lowered a bare lightbulb hanging on a rope and pulled a threaded needle through my skin. I felt the air begin to vibrate around my head. When I opened my eyes briefly, Soojin was there, leaning down, stroking my ear before my body shook and I passed out.

Every now and then I spotted a uniformed woman with her long hair braided, taking her hat off and ducking into a tent, and my ears and tail would lift, the sudden relief of a familiar person flooding into me, and I let out a whine, wanting to run to her, but Fuji would nip my shoulder lightly and tell me to remember my training.

Who would've believed it if I told them that Fuji would end up larger and stronger than me? That she would be the one who led us dogs, who charged into places first, who took the first step onto an unknown road? She was the one who fought the fiercest. Who was braver than the rest of us. Who fought and kept fighting.

But on that first day together, Fuji had been much more frightened than I was. *Are we a pack now?* she nervously asked as Soojin departed and the men slipped us into crates beside each other on the back of another truck. When they, too, were gone, when the truck started and we sped down another road, Fuji shifted over in her crate to be as close to me as possible.

I did the same, pressing my snout against my own crate until I could almost feel her damp nose against mine. The mole on the tip of her tongue whenever she tried to lick me. Her alert eyes, which were bright blue, staring back.

Are we a pack now?

From the gas station that afternoon, we kept traveling. We traveled far. Nights and nights. Eventually we ended up at an American base, where we stayed for five months and trained and learned commands in English, along with some German and French in case we would be working with the Germans or the French.

We met many other dogs.

Every day was the opposite of the farm. Every day became more new noises and new voices and concrete and dirt and the smell of fuel and human piss and shit and what I would quickly discover to be the variety of smells of explosives and gunpowder.

But every day there were also the dogs. There was Fuji beside me, working alongside me. There was Fuji napping or resting nearby as airplanes and helicopters landed and took off. How, to keep our minds busy, we would talk to each other about what we did well that morning and what frightened us. Or, sometimes, in our exhaustion, we would just lie there, silently thinking of our homes and what was happening there, as we looked across at each other the way we did in those crates in that truck.

Every day we tried not to wonder about what the hours would bring. Where we might go and what we would have to do.

Every day we worked with our handlers. Each dog was assigned one. The one assigned to me was named Jason. He was around Soojin's age, but shorter than she was, with thick palms and short, dark hair. He knew how to speak a little in this country's language, but he spoke mostly in English to me, which I learned to understand.

I found myself being drawn to Jason immediately. I found comfort in his steady hands and the way he knelt to greet me, smiling and saying *Etna* to me not once, but three times—*Etna, Etna, Etna*—like he was gently but firmly pulling on a line of string.

Even in those early weeks when I was with Jason, it was like he knew how to form a perimeter around only us, which I grew to feel more and more comfortable moving and existing in.

I saw Fuji, a few meters away, feel the same about her handler, Brian, who was a giant, with giant laughter, as the two of them trained the way Jason and I trained, all those pairs of us—human and dog—in our own moving circles on that base.

I learned to move when Jason told me to move. To keep still when he told me to keep still. Then the perimeter extended, and I ran when he told me to run. I ran across fields and up slopes, and I came back to him. I slowed when he told me to slow, and then he held small containers with different smells, and I learned to seek out those smells in those fields.

I entered buildings they had constructed on the base without ceilings so that people in their uniforms could watch me from the rafters. I moved from room to room, ears up, nose to the ground. I learned to rush someone from the back, leap, and lock my jaw onto their arm and pull them down with momentum and speed. I learned to locate men who were hiding in those rooms and run back outside into those fields to locate others who were running away, and I learned to run faster. I learned what to listen for and what to smell out: nicotine and sweat; urine and gunpowder; the hum of an electrical current like in a battery or a SIM card; the weight of a foot on a floorboard.

I learned to attack a particular artery in the thigh or go for the genitals or the throat, and to jump onto backs of pickup trucks and through open car windows and attack whoever was sitting inside.

I learned the shapes of weapons and to avoid the heat of barrels after weapons had been discharged.

I grew used to people touching my legs and paws until it was nothing to me.

And eating fast. And endless, simultaneous voices. And explosions. And gunfire. And all the shouting. And sections of those fields cracking open and lifting up as airplanes sped by overhead. I grew used to running across those fields cracking open. And to coming back to Jason, to heel beside him and watch Fuji and the other dogs come back to their own handlers, and for us to do this all over again.

I saw other dogs land in the wrong way or simply stop swimming across the manmade pond, too exhausted, the small islands of their ears and noses reflecting daylight for a moment before they went under.

I saw my shadow become taller and thicker and faster.

During those months, I thought I would return home in dreams, to the farm and the coast, or perhaps even find Soojin there, but all I ever dreamed about were fields. And small islands across those fields. I kept staring, waiting, until Fuji, who often slept beside me, placed her paw on my paw and broke me away from those dreams.

Days moved like water. Over and over again.

In the barracks where we all slept, someone said that maybe the war would be over by the time we were finished with our training. But the war didn't end, it only got worse and spread, and so after those months, they divided all of us up by what we were best at.

Fuji and I stuck together because we were better at the same thing, so we—us and our handlers—joined up with a group of sappers and engineers. We became a unit that consisted of two other dogs and twelve men, and we were sent to regions that had been bombed or that the country had fought to take back. We sniffed out land mines and hidden, improvised devices and ordnances that hadn't detonated when they struck the ground. We stood guard together, listening for anything approaching us from the distance while Jason, Brian, and the other men blew up the mines remotely or defused them by hand. We cleared houses and towns and roads or figured out a way to make new, passable roads for our troops and supplies.

We worked and fought all over the country. We walked and ran and trekked and rode in trucks and jumped through open and broken windows and we climbed and ascended and we lived almost every day with explosions and gunfire and houses falling and buildings falling and animals running and everywhere fire and bodies on fire and the earth breaking and breaking deeper; and Jason and Brian and all the men we were with killed other men and sometimes animals, and I killed, and Fuji killed, and the other dogs killed.

We lost men. We lost dogs. We met up with more men and their dogs from other units, and we worked and traveled and fought and killed.

We slept when and where we could. We slept in the remnants of houses and beside the remnants of trees and in rain and snow, and some nights when it was safe and silent, we watched the men build their own fires on top of the earth that had already been burned by fires, and we all slept beside those new fires and woke and got up and started again.

Four years.

I got injured six times. Most times it was only the graze of shrapnel or a bullet or something else small and sharp. Each time not enough to leave Jason, Fuji, and our unit permanently, but enough to send me to a medic or a doctor to get patched up.

Fuji: she got injured five times.

As time went on, the more hurt she was, the more she wanted to hurt.

And the blue in her eyes grew less blue, and I could never explain that.

I saw the coast twice, but it wasn't mine.

Stripes of scars like old worms grew across my forehead and along my sides.

I stopped staring at my shadow.

It was in the third year, while we were on furlough in the mountains, when Fuji ran off one morning. Without warning, without explanation. Without telling me where she was going. If she knew where she was going.

I never saw Fuji again.

Early the following year, in what would be the last year of the war, Brian made a mistake as he attempted to help defuse a set of anti-tank mines we had been ordered to clear for supply trucks passing through. I was nearby with Jason, having sniffed out another mine the unit had missed. Jason was humming a song to distract himself from his exhaustion and the cold.

In the same moment I heard a metallic click in the ground, like a tiny vibration, Brian turned, I saw his breath bloom white in the cold, and I saw his frightened eyes as he shouted at Jason, who without hesitation grabbed my scruff, lifted me up into his arms like I was a puppy again, and began to run.

Jason, whose hands grew less steady as the war went on. Who, as he ran carrying me, counted the four seconds out loud like he was counting his last heartbeats before he threw me as far as he could, extending his arms to form as wide of a shield as possible as his body blew apart.

In the end, I lost all three of them: Fuji and Jason and giant Brian.

They had been beside me almost every moment from those first days, never far until they were.

Over a thousand sunsets and sunrises. Over a thousand moons.

And how there was never a choice after but to follow orders and to keep moving and going and working.

By the time the fighting stopped across this country, I was the only dog left from our original unit.

Maybe I was thinking of this fact—that I was the only dog left—when the last two remaining men in our unit and I returned to the American base where I had trained. Or maybe it was Fuji's vanishing I was thinking of.

It was late summer. The evening was clear and cool. All the doors had been left open and all the people on the base were celebrating the end of the war. A speech was given in the mess hall and, later, I could hear singing and kissing. Music on speakers. The smell of meat on a grill. Headlights were on in a lot right outside the barracks doors, and someone was trying to film someone else dancing, the manic silhouette of limbs and a body.

Four men stumbled through a far field I used to run back and forth across. I could hear their bootlaces catching on the overgrown blades of grass. They turned on a few large drones—I caught the low, whirring hum of them cutting through the night as one of the men lifted his handgun into the night sky and fired until someone rushed out of a building and reprimanded them.

Afterward, the night grew calmer. I was lying on the floor between the two surviving men in my unit. They were set to return to their homes. They were on their cots, side by side, wondering what they were going to do with me, now that it was over. They mentioned that they didn't even know where I had come from, or couldn't remember anymore, there was no paperwork they could find.

Their conversation moved from me to a movie they wanted to see, to some money one of them had buried in their backyard before they had come to this country. The other asked why, but they were drunk, passing the bottle over my head. A drop hit my paw, and I watched the bead of dark liquid slip down to the ground, where it mixed with some old semen and leather and the remains of a bee's wing.

The one on my left said that he wanted nothing to do with this place at all.

And that includes him, he said, pointing down at me.

Music came from the far side of the room.

The other thought he should bring me back home to California with him.

I remembered him talking about California a few times before. I remembered because he talked about a coast in the place called California, about sand and birds and other animals and farms on this coast.

But I could tell in his voice that he didn't mean what he had just said about taking me with him. I wasn't his dog. When he saw me, he saw the dog he had worked with and fought alongside and lost.

For a while, there was silence, only their breathing. Then the first said that none of us were right in the head after what we saw and did and what our bodies and souls endured. And that the best thing would be to put me out of my misery.

What's left here to go back to anyway? he said. How will he survive? It's a total wasteland. Completely ruined. When was the last time you saw a standing building? An animal other than a mangy cat or a half-dead, starving dog?

Yeah, we sort of made a mess of things here, didn't we?

Godzilla versus Kong, he said.

Who was Godzilla and who was Kong? the other said.

They chuckled. They got quiet again and drank.

I turned and got up to stretch. They ignored me. I looked around at the other cots and I didn't think too much about what I did next. I remembered that I had come to this base when I was a year old, and now I was five. I was neither young nor old. These two men were young humans, only twenty-seven and twenty-nine. I didn't blame them for anything they did or said. They had been good to their dogs.

Everyone wanted to go home. And to go away.

In that moment, I realized I wanted this, too. To go away. To go home.

It seemed possible, suddenly, that the farm might still be there. Or that something might still be there.

As soon as I thought this, I knew it was impossible.

And yet, I kept thinking about it.

Wondering if, perhaps, this was what Fuji had wanted, too, when she vanished: to be somewhere outside of all these years. But where that place was for her, I couldn't say. (As the war went on, she had stopped talking about where she was from.)

For me, it was the farm. It had always been the farm and the coast.

I wanted to go home.

So I left the American base later that night while everyone was sleeping. With nothing, not even my vest or my collar. I ate all the food the two men had dropped on the floor. I drank the rest of the water in my bowl.

I walked out of the barracks toward the sentries posted at the gate. I lowered my head and walked under the roadblock, and they just watched and whistled. They shook their heads and one of them said, Poor bastard, look at the shape he's in. Is that his fur? Jesus.

That's a zombie dog, another said.

I lifted my head and caught anxiety and exhaustion in their eyes. I wondered where home was for them. I thought *Godzilla* and *Kong*, and growled a little. I didn't think they heard me, but they stepped back and didn't stop me, they just kept watching. I could feel them watching as I stepped across the perimeter of the spotlights and entered the night.

I walked for a long time. I walked slowly but steadily. I walked all night on the side of a dirt road, veering off into the grass whenever I heard a military truck approaching.

I walked until I came to a fork where one road was traversable by vehicles; the other had been bombed out, but I could still see the outline of it in the approaching dawn.

I took the bombed-out road. I climbed up and down the new shapes of earth that had hardened and dried. Pieces of old grass stuck out of them like hair.

I climbed down craters where there were pieces of rubber tires, rusted metal, and old feathers from blackbirds. I heard jet engines overhead but only saw the sky. Some stars. A long purple cloud.

The road eventually led into the woods—or what had been the woods. Most of the trees on each side had burned to their stumps. I left the road as first light appeared and I found some other trees that had collapsed into the shape of a shelter. I was about to slide under and rest when a wind came and I heard the tilt of something metal over leaves, a brief crunching sound.

I remembered a goat on the farm, but the image vanished like the way fog always vanished as I walked through it, the damp sticking to my coat.

I searched out the noise until I found an overturned soldier's helmet against the base of a tree. The helmet was filled with rainwater, which I sniffed, avoiding my own reflection. I decided to drink the water.

These days, water from the sky tasted like exhaust from the fighter jets. (I got used to that.)

I waited to feel sick. When I didn't, I drank the rest.

I returned to the tree shelter and slid under and lay down with my head on my paws, trying not to think of food. My eyes grew heavy as I kept watch on the bombed-out road and the thin, bare trees that remained standing.

No one. Nothing. No birds. Just more engines somewhere faroff, and then the air shifted and I was suddenly in front of an old well in a clearing, watching leaves spin down its mouth.

I was convinced the leaves would fly back up.

So I jumped up against the mouth of the well, like a goat, then peered down and waited.

When I woke up, the day had passed and it was dark again. I drank what was left of the water in the helmet and kept going. I walked all through another night and found another tree shelter and stayed there and rested.

I sniffed out a mouse that had died not long ago. I didn't know how long, there were no wounds on it, and it smelled all right, so I ate it.

I waited to get sick. I didn't.

I walked on, and in the afternoon I saw in the distance a figure pulling a large, empty wooden cart along the bombed-out road. He had a harness on him, and he was strapped to the cart as if he were a horse or a donkey.

I approached carefully, wondering if he might have food. I stayed silent.

Then I froze because I smelled what the empty cart had been carrying.

I was about to turn back, but the man spotted me. His shirt was open and hanging loose about him like a coat. There were cuts all over his chest that hadn't healed, knife cuts, I thought, and his ribs were more visible than mine.

His eyes widened as he opened his mouth like a child and took off his straw hat and whipped it in the air. And then he began to shout for me to come to him, to please come, and when I didn't, he screamed up into the air. I thought he would take the harness off and run after me, but he kept the harness on and kept screaming and waving his hat as I ran back into the woods.

I ran until I couldn't hear him. I only stopped when I grew tired and hot, and I panted and could feel the mouse digesting inside, and I worried again that I was going to be sick. But I didn't get sick, and I was glad because I didn't want to throw the mouse up.

I found a stream. I listened around me. I drank from the stream, then I stepped in, feeling the water on my paws and my legs. The water felt good. I thought, why not, and lay down in the shallows.

The water cooled me. I listened to the water moving past me and clinging to my fur. I drank some more and lay there until I stopped panting, and then I got up and followed the stream until it grew dark again.

The water turned the color of the moon in places.

Every time I stepped in those places, the moon broke, and I didn't mind watching that. I pawed the water, the moon broke. I did this for a while, lost in the wavering, silver light.

It was like the valley floor where we had left Jason. In my mind he was there, tonight, forever grabbing my scruff and running and throwing me as far as he could.

Some days, I could still feel his hands on my neck like that.

And the spaces appearing between parts of his body where there shouldn't have been spaces.

And the small pieces of his bones that had shot into my skin when the mine exploded.

Like the hint of teeth from my mother when I was a pup, when she would lift me up by her mouth to quiet me.

My mother. I didn't know how to explain it, but even though I no longer remembered her and my siblings that well, the farthest and faintest layer of their scents sometimes came to me, on the wind, briefly, which made me understand that they were no longer in their bodies, that they were no longer alive.

Still, I wanted to return to the farm. I wanted to go home. I wanted to see what was there.

I pawed the night water, the moon broke.

In the morning, I arrived at a field. An enormous, overgrown field.

I stood by the tree line. Across the tall grass stood a low, wide building with a thatched roof. Open windows. I couldn't tell what kind of building it was.

I sat, ears up and forward. The grass almost to my chest as I latched on to a distant sound. It was coming from the other side of the building. The sound was movement—it was smooth and rhythmic, almost like the movement of a horse, though it was much lighter, softer, no hooves.

Maybe I was thinking of a horse because of the man who had harnessed himself to a cart. Or maybe I was thinking of all the animals I had not seen in a long time.

I sniffed the air, but all I smelled from here was the earth. Age. Wood.

There was nothing else in the field. Also nothing, I didn't think, inside the building. Save for that unknown noise, I could only hear the occasional wind passing through, the light rattle of a sliding door.

I glanced back into the woods in the direction of the stream from the night before. I thought I could wait under one of the fallen trees again until I could figure out what the sound was.

But then the sound stopped. I waited to see if it would pick up again.

Silence. The wind.

I decided to leave the tree line and approach. But the field grass was not only tall but thick. It was grass that nothing had crossed over in a long time. I couldn't always see where my paws were touching, so I kept my nose as close to the ground as possible, and I stepped carefully and very slowly, trying not to bend the grass too much in case I was heard.

The Americans taught me this: Explosives had vapors. Even buried ones. The vapors came up through the soil. Vapors of explosives smelled sweet like the sugar in chewing gum or the toothpaste Jason used to use.

(I always loved the smell of toothpaste.)

There were no explosives in this area of the field. There was the smell of the night rain that had already evaporated, some fur from a mole, dead leaves, stones, gunpowder, the microchip of a drone, old blood. From at least a year ago.

The noise picked up again.

I stopped, but I was too close now. If it was an animal, it would have already smelled me. I lowered my head, shoulders up as I rounded the building, the rot smell of the thatch all around, the clatter of bare trees high above.

When I reached the other side, I was surprised to find a dog there, pacing. Or trying to.

He was very old. I could already see that. He was larger than I was, but thinner, with a dark coat, and he was pacing in a circle in what was the front of the building. He wasn't far from the front doors of the building, which were ajar, the space wide enough for us to fit through.

I wasn't sure if the dog had noticed me yet. He had been walking so much he had formed a shallow, circular trench in the grass. I didn't know how long it must've taken him to do that.

He kept circling as I approached. Then he slowly lay down, panting, facing away from me.

I moved in front of him, lay down, and said hello.

He tilted his head back and hung on to my voice. I could now make out the cataracts all over his eyes. The milky white. And his disfigured nose. It had been wounded in some way and had scarred over and now resembled a piece of ginger root growing on his snout.

He said, Where are you?

I crawled closer, and he said, Are you real?

Last time I checked, I said.

He softened his brow, which was how dogs smiled. He let me smell him. He seemed to find pleasure in my smelling him. His tail wagged and thumped on the ground. He opened his mouth. There was some blood on his gums. I thought maybe he had managed to kill an animal, but the blood was his own.

I can't smell very well anymore, he said. But that happened a long time ago. This, this is new.

He was referring to his eyes. He ran his face over mine, then along my shoulders, taking in the shape of me. I let him, feeling his disfigured nose on me. It had been a while since I had interacted with another dog. If he sensed my scars, he didn't say, he just kept smiling.

I asked if he had any water, and he aimed his snout toward a bowl near the front door. I rushed over, sniffed, and drank. I almost drank all of it, then apologized. I asked him his name. He said he didn't have one.

All dogs had private names. They were the names our mothers called us by, but we never shared those or asked each other about them. In the first year of the war, I would catch myself saying mine over again as I kept startling myself awake, and I wondered if Fuji ever heard. If she did, she never mentioned it.

I turned away from the old dog, droplets of water falling from my mouth onto the dirt, and I stared up at the building. I didn't think it was a house, or any kind of house I had ever seen.

A cobweb hung in one of the window frames, trembling, catching the sun.

I asked what he was doing there in the grass, and he tilted his head back again as though he didn't realize what it was he had been doing.

From the far, opposite tree line came the sound of more faraway jets. A moment later, a breeze passed over the field.

Are you alone? I asked.

He said, Are you?

I said I was. But I told him about the man I saw with the cart and asked if he knew anything about that. He didn't answer that question, either.

I looked high above us and asked if there were any birds around.

Birds? You mean, to eat?

No. I meant had he noticed any flying about? I told him it felt like I hadn't seen a bird in years.

He lay down again where he had been standing, the front part of him going first, followed by his hind legs.

Now that you mention it, he said, but didn't go on. Instead, he said, Are you from the city?

The city? I said. Is there a city nearby?

A few days' walk, he said. You can follow the tracks.

Tracks?

With his disfigured nose, he pointed to the opposite tree line, across the portion of the field that the front of the house was facing. Behind those trees, I could see now, lay a platform. And beyond that, a range of mountains, where the jets I had heard were gliding over.

Have the mountain trees grown back?

I couldn't tell from here.

They all burned, the dog said, sensing that I was staring out into the distance. Those mountains. They burned.

I know it, I said.

And I did. I had seen mountains burn. I had seen lakes burn and boulders burn and airplanes burn and tanks burn and animals burn and humans burn and bones burn. And when there was nothing left to burn, there was still the sound of it. I would always remember the sound of the burning.

If I had a choice, I thought, I would rather step on a mine.

Are you from the city? the dog asked again.

I was about to say he had already asked me that, but I just said again that I wasn't.

The old dog said that he had been born in the city, but he didn't remember much of it anymore. He said that he remembered being excited whenever he took walks, the infinite smells of the sidewalks, the hundreds and hundreds of shoe soles and where those shoes had been, all the trash bins, the surprise and delight of seeing your reflection in a puddle of rain, a storefront window.

I asked how long ago that was, but again, he didn't respond.

I was wondering what this building was near the train tracks when the dog said, I'm sorry. I haven't talked to a dog in a while, I forget how long. I'm going on and on. I forgot . . . is it over? Nothing's happened here in a while. No one's passed through. Nothing else has burned.

I told him it was over. That the fighting was over.

Did we win? the old dog asked.

I glanced back at the bare forest I had come out of. I thought about Jason in the valley. I thought about the people celebrating at the base, each of them talking about going home. The dancer. The drones. I thought about the two men in my unit, lying on their cots, but couldn't recall now how many days ago all that was.

—

Yes, I said. I suppose we did win.

Oh, the dog said. That's good. They would want to know that.

They?

I stiffened my spine. I turned quickly to face the door. It was ajar, but I heard nothing inside. I smelled nothing inside.

Then I remembered the men talking about everyone not being right in the head. Maybe the old dog wasn't right in the head. And then I wondered what part of my own head might not be right without my knowing.

Are you hungry? he said.

Are you joking? I said.

He smiled again. He said, Head over to the tree line. Take a left at the platform. You'll see some train cars. Go to the middle one. You'll find a surprise. I'd go with you but I'm too tired. I'll wait for you here. Bring some back for me, will you?

I hesitated, smelling the air, ears up.

Go on, he said. It's safe. I promise.

His eyes grew heavy. He rested his head on his paws, and I watched as he fell asleep.

I got up and walked across the field toward the platform. I found where a path had been, a wide dirt path that had long overgrown. I followed that until I passed the thin line of trees and walked onto the platform. It was empty except for a set of steel steps by the track, curving up into the air, waiting for a train that wasn't coming.

From where I stood, it appeared as though it were a ladder for the distant mountains. I heard the jets again, faintly, but couldn't see them.

It was then I caught a small bright flash on top of the mountain range. It was like the flash of a faraway weapon, and I waited for a noise to echo toward me.

But there was no noise. I lifted my nose into the air, inhaling deeply: old metal; damp wood; a struggling flower.

Azalea.

I heard that word years ago from somebody. I liked the length of the word. The way it stayed in you for a little longer than it should.

I waited for another flash, but none came.

I moved to the left, following the pieces of what was left of the tracks. Up ahead lay a few train cars, overturned. The last one was completely severed in half. Broken benches and glass were strewn about the ground.

I headed to the middle one, which could be accessed by a hole in what had been the roof of the train car.

I could smell something rotten. I peered in without entering at first, waiting for my eyes to focus inside the dark of the train car.

Soon, I could make out crates and boxes. Heaps and heaps of crates and boxes. They were all open or shattered or flipped on their side. Spilling out of them were unopened white boxes with new phones in them as well as boxes of what I knew were tiny drones the size of chestnuts like the ones my unit had used.

Against the opposite wall, in a pile, were boxes of wrapped crackers and tins of meat. Some of the tins the old dog had torn open and eaten what he could. The remaining meat in the open tins had spoiled—that was what I had smelled—and mice had gotten to them.

I understood why his gums were bleeding now, but I didn't care. I went for the crackers first and then I grabbed a tin, pawed it, and bit into it. I made a hole wide enough for me to lick the tinned meat. I kept licking the salt and fat and tore a bigger hole and took a bite of the meat and ate some more. I drooled all over the tin. I ate what I could reach with my tongue and teeth, and I tore open another one.

A loud bang filled the car.

I jumped, lowered myself, ready to lunge. But it was just the old dog. He had hit himself against the wall and was standing there by the entrance, shaking on his legs a little.

I kept eating and asked if everything was all right.

I thought, the dog said. I woke up . . . and I thought you had been a dream.

I went over and nudged him to turn around. I said that maybe we should go back. In case anyone heard that noise.

He said, Okay. Is it getting dark?

It was daytime. But I said, Yes, it's getting dark, and I grabbed another tin of meat with my mouth, and we stepped out of the train car, and I led him back.

I returned to the train car a few more times. I tore open what I could, and I ate, and I gave some to the old dog.

He thanked me but he didn't eat much. He paced a little in his circle, lay down, slept, and paced again.

I walked over to the building wall, under the rotting eaves, and rested. From here, I had a view of the dog and the train platform. From here, I would also be able to hear if something or someone came out of the woods behind us, from where I had come out. If that man with the scars all over him and the crate appeared again. But if he had been following me, I would've smelled him. I kept telling myself that until I no longer thought about the man.

I thought about how I once saw, from a great distance, a young black bear running away from a column of tanks. The lead tank swiveled and fired and then the tanks kept going to wherever they were heading.

I thought about how the men in our unit kept hurrying up the slope we had been climbing and how we—the dogs—hurried up, too, beside them, not turning around, forcing ourselves not to turn around.

That was the last bear I saw. I had not seen an animal that could overpower me in a long time. Just men. Vehicles. A bullet.

I pressed myself against the building wall and kept watch and listened. My belly was full. Only when it was silent for long enough, with the old dog's heavy breathing, did I curl up and sleep.

I dreamed of the well, but this time it wasn't leaves falling, but feathers, and I watched as an enormous bird hovered over me against the sunlight, staring down.

I startled awake. Across from me, the old dog was standing and pissing. I got up to smell his piss. I could smell the tinned meat and the soil and his old age. And then I pissed, too. It was not yet dark. I could tell he had been waiting for me to get up.

I ate some more, and I asked if he knew if the southeastern coast was nearby.

He asked if that was where I was trying to get to. I nodded, then remembered he couldn't see. I said, Yes, I'm trying to get to the coast. To the sea.

I said that I was trying to get home.

I could tell the old dog was about to ask me something, but he paused. He lifted his snout and thought. He licked his paws and said that he didn't know if the southeastern coast was nearby.

But he said someone in the city might know, and I agreed.

Then he asked if the humans had named me, and I told him.

Etna? he said, trying to pronounce it.

I said it was the name of a volcano.

What's a volcano? he said.

His ears moved as I explained it as best as I knew. I said it was like a door holding in what was inside the earth. And sometimes that door broke open, and the earth erupted and there was fire.

You mean war? the old dog said. You're named after war?

I stayed quiet. I licked my paw. No one had ever said that about my name before.

I licked my other paw. I watched the first star appear in the sky. I waited for any signs of birds.

The dog asked how I had survived the years. I didn't feel like talking about it, but he had showed me where the food was. My belly was full. So I told him. I told him about what I did. I told him about the base where I had trained and my unit and the towns and the roads we cleared and the new roads we made and the ambushes and the fighting and all the traveling up and down this country and all the people refusing to leave their homes even though there were no homes surrounding them, only a part of a wall or a chimney flue or the chair they refused to get out of, and everywhere the dead cats and the dead dogs.

The old dog's ears moved again as I talked. I grew self-conscious of how much I had been talking, and then Fuji came into my mind again, which made me stop.

You found your purpose, the dog said.

I thought about how to answer that. I said, I learned to be good at it.

Which part?

All of it, I said.

The old dog considered this. He got up, paced a little, and lay back down. I wasn't certain if it was because he had eaten food, but there was a clarity to him now. Or maybe it depended on the time of day.

He cleared his throat and told me the building I had slept against used to be a way station for travelers. They would get off at the platform and walk the path to the building.

He had been the way station owners' dog. That was his purpose, he said. To keep guard of the station and the family who lived here. A husband and a wife, at first. Then a child. The wife made food for the travelers and there were three guest rooms if anyone needed to spend the night before venturing farther into the country by taxi or a connecting train.

If a traveler liked animals, the dog got to stay inside. But most nights he was in front of the door, guarding the place. There had been a small stable for mules and donkeys. Chickens.

The owners didn't leave right away. Because the trains were still running during those first days. And by the time the owners thought of leaving, this country's army came, wanting to use the station. They blocked off everything: no more accessible roads; no one going in or out.

And that was how the family ended up staying and not heading farther south. It all happened so quickly. For a time, the owners took care of the soldiers. The soldiers, in a strange but wonderful moment of distraction, helped take care of the child.

There were moments when it felt like there was no war, the old dog said. When a soldier would sing to the child to try to get the child to sleep; or the child would steal their hats and leave them all over the field, and we would stumble upon them throughout the day like they were flowers; or a group would sit outside facing the mountains like it was any other day, like they were waiting for a train to bring them to the city.

The dog went on: Eventually, of course, the fighting came here. Terrible fighting. The tracks were bombed. The trees. Men came. Tanks came. Jets. And then it was all done. Or passed through. It all just passed. Like wind. The days. Time.

But I never left, he said. I never ran away.

He said this with pride. And then the pride vanished, and he licked his paws.

He said, One of the bombs—I think it was one of the bombs. Something hit my face. The last thing I remember was everyone running into the fields and me trying to follow them. The husband in one direction. In the other, the wife carrying the child. If they were talking or shouting, I couldn't hear. They just ran. Desperate, panicked running. And then . . . fire . . . volcano. Is that what you call it? Volcano?

The dog paused. I can't smell very well anymore, he said. Did I already tell you that? I think I would have found them long ago if I were able to smell. I crawled back to the building, and I didn't leave it for a very long time. I don't know how long. Then I stepped out and tried to find them, but I couldn't find anything. It was just the field. The broken field. I couldn't smell anything.

And then the days passed. The months. Years? The grass regrew. And now my eyes. I'll never be able to find them with these eyes.

I don't understand, I said.

I was listening to him, but I wasn't following what he was saying.

I want you to find them, the dog said.

Find them?

In the field. Find them for me. The man, the woman, and the child.

I hesitated.

They are in the field, he said.

I asked how he knew.

Just try, he said. Please. Please just try.

He said again, Please. I'm so tired. I keep trying. I can't find them. Find them. Please. Please just try.

I wanted to know which room the family slept in. He told me to enter the building and swing right, that I would find their room at the end.

I asked if he could come with me to show me, but he shook his head and said that he didn't want to go in there anymore.

I thought that meant there would be men in there, lying there, from the years, but I went in and found the building to be entirely empty. It was almost dark, but I could make out the corridors and even the small outdoor courtyard where there were the remnants of a garden and pieces of what had been a stone statue at the center.

A pool of water reflected the first star of the night I saw earlier.

I listened. I smelled. I moved lightly.

Like the train cars, there was evidence of a firefight, but nothing unexpected. The paper on the sliding doors was shredded, hanging like tiny flags, dull from the weather. Pieces of the floorboards were gone.

Some framed art on the hallway wall had fallen and shattered and were now replaced by their ghosts, squares of a paler shade than the walls themselves.

There were water stains from the open windows and the leaking roof. Shattered teapots and cups and televisions and phones.

On a low table, there was a dried-out foot of a pig someone had saved as a keepsake of some kind. I almost licked it and put it in my mouth but remembered my training.

I smelled deeply, but mostly it was the smell of the outside, but inside. The air. The seasons. Stone dust and ground dust and wood dust and sun dust and cloud dust. That cobweb I had seen earlier holding old rain and jet fuel dust.

I jumped over a gap in the floor and headed into the last room. There was a pair of rolled-up mats in the corner. A computer with a cracked screen on a desk. Beside the desk was a dresser with its door hanging open. Inside, I spotted some clothes, and I went there, but only smelled the wood of the furniture.

Then I saw the hairbrush on a shelf.

That was a different smell. I held on to that smell.

I returned to the hall, and the hairbrush smell led me back to the pig's foot. And then to a wall and then to the statue in the garden.

I went outside. It was dark now, but there was the moon. The light was spread all over. Clean light. I could see the entire field.

The dog was lying down but awake, listening to me. Nose to the ground, I started by swinging right and moving in a zigzag. I checked for explosives here, too, but there were none.

I reached the tree line and returned, and I did it again until I was behind the house, not far from where I had emerged from the woods. I paused briefly to scan the woods again, listening, but there were no strange sounds. I kept searching, pushing through the thick, tall grass, inhaling and exhaling, swinging my nose across the ground.

I worked fast, and for a moment forgot where I was and what I was searching for. I was working. It was different work, but it was work, and it was work I knew how to do. The inhaling and my limbs moving and everything like a fog I was sifting through to unearth a strong, clear line that was a single smell.

I felt the pleasure of this. I held the hairbrush smell and kept searching.

I had almost come around to the other side, the left side of the house, when I walked over the same hairbrush smell, or thought I did.

I turned and circled, nose nearly touching the ground, and then my nose touched something hard sticking up slightly in the ground.

I smelled deeply. Then I pawed the ground around the hard thing and kept pawing until I could grip the thing with my teeth. I pulled it out of the dirt and saw in the moonlight that it was a jaw, or a piece of a lower jaw, and I kept pawing and digging.

I couldn't find anything else. I carried the jaw over to the dog, who was awake and alert, lying in the trench circle he had made. I dropped the jaw in front of him, and he pawed it and leaned his face against it.

He said, Oh, who did you find?

I didn't know. I mentioned the hairbrush I had found, and he said, Yes, that's it, yes, and he held the jaw between his paws and began to wail.

The wailing startled me. I told him to keep quiet, that we didn't know if anyone was nearby, and he said, Yes, yes. He apologized. He licked the jaw and said, Keep looking, keep looking.

I kept looking. I couldn't find anything else in that area, so I went back into the house, into that room, and found another smell that was different, on the insole of a shoe, and walked the field all over again.

I did this all night. I worked the field and found two long bones, side by side, not far from the train platform.

Then near those long bones, I found a skull.

I brought all those over to the dog and searched all over again.

He had told me there were three humans, a man, woman, and child, but I could only find two. I found a buried rifle and a soldier's boot. A drone. A belt buckle and bullet casings and crushed phones and eyeglasses and a ring.

The sun came up. The top of the mountains brightened. Then the trees and the field.

I didn't find any more skulls or bones. I went back around and told him. I drank the rest of the water that had been in the bowl and lay down.

I said, There're only two.

And he said, Are you sure?

Only two I can find, I said.

I shut my eyes. I heard the dog stand and gather together the bones and the skull with what was left of his nose, and he lay back down beside them.

I heard him say, Thank you, thank you so much, and I said that I needed to rest for a little bit. He kept saying thank you, and I pressed myself against the wall, feeling the sun, and slept.

No dream this time.

But then, waking, forgetting for a moment where I was, a memory:

In that mountain town in the third year of the war, Brian, Jason, and I had been walking around the town, searching for Fuji. I could smell her on occasion, in an air current. I was moving quickly, sometimes too quickly, and whimpering so that Jason had to tell me to stop. But in the end, she had traversed the area in a way that had confused me.

In the town that day, a train appeared. Going so slow I could walk alongside it. A soldier slid open a car window. The men in my unit asked if anyone had seen a loose dog. The soldier shook his head and threw a letter at Jason, asking if he would post it for him. Jason slid it into his shirt pocket, and we watched the train speed up and leave the mountain.

I remembered thinking of the possibility that Fuji had jumped onto the train. She was nimble, almost silent whenever she jumped. I also remembered thinking of this possibility because it occurred to me that I could jump on the train, too. Right there and then. It didn't have anything to do with the unit I belonged to, or Jason, or even wanting to find Fuji. It was just a passing thought.

Even then, the near-uncontrollable desire to jump. To go.

But I would've told Fuji, I thought. I would've asked her to come.

I was better than her, I thought.

I opened my eyes to the empty train platform down the path. The sun was strong and casting shadows of the building eaves.

I was trying to remember what Jason did with that letter, when I noticed the old dog wasn't in the circle he had made. Only the bones I had found were there. The skull staring back at me.

I sat up and listened. The wind. A piece of tin rolling in the wind. Branches. Grass. Shredded paper. Then I located his breathing and went inside.

He was in the courtyard, sitting by the remnants of the stone statue. He heard me, I saw his ears perk up, but he didn't turn around.

There used to be fish here in the pond, he said. I got in trouble once for eating one. I wasn't allowed back in for a while.

He tucked his head down. I sat beside him in the garden.

He said, I think I'll come back inside, now that you found them. It's comfortable in here, in the shade.

I reminded him that I had only found two. That they were the only ones I could find.

Oh yes, he said. Oh yes, but you found two.

I could feel his breath on me. I told him I knew a dog who was better at this than I was. But that she had vanished in the mountains one year.

Then I described her and asked if he had ever run into her. He said he never had.

A cloud shadow moved over the courtyard.

He said, Do you think it's possible?

Possible?

That one of them made it out of the field. One of the three family members. The man, the woman, maybe even the child.

I had no idea. I didn't think so. I said that in all the years, I had never seen a human outrun human weapons. Not a single animal, either.

Yes, he said. That must be right. Except you.

Except me what? I said.

You outran them, the dog said. The weapons.

I hesitated. I lifted a back paw to scratch my elbow. I could feel each scar on my coat, each worm squirming through and under me. I remembered the old dog's face moving over me, knowing he would never know what I looked like.

No, I said to him. I never outran them.

Me neither, he said, and softened his brow. Did you get some rest? While you were here?

I had.

Then he said, You're going today, I can tell. You can stay, of course, but I know you're going.

I was going.

Do you think it's still there? he said.

I knew immediately that he meant my home. And I understood that he had been wanting to ask me that for a while.

Before I could respond, though, he said, I hope you find it. Your coast. Home.

Yes, I said.

But if you don't, he said. Or if it's not there, this will be here. Not me. I'll be gone by then. But this shelter will be here. Remember that. You can always come back. This will be here.

You will be here, I said, knowing it probably wasn't true. Knowing that he was right. I also knew that I shouldn't have said that. I was like Jason and Brian, who kept telling each other every day that everything was going to be all right.

But the old dog didn't seem bothered. He scratched his front leg with his hind paw, lay down, and stretched his body out across the courtyard.

There's no place for us here anymore, is there? he said.

What do you mean? I said.

In what comes next, he said. Here. Whatever comes next. After all this. Where do we fit in? But maybe there never was a place for us here.

This time, we heard large trucks in the far distance.

I thought about what he had said. Then I said, There's no other place but here.

He seemed satisfied with my response. Yes, he said again. Yes, that must be right.

He thanked me for my help again. He thanked me for finding them. He thanked me for the company and for the conversations, and he thanked me for letting him know that it was over.

I licked his face. He shut his eyes, and I licked his face again.

You could listen to my heart, he said. If you want.

It had been a long time since an animal had said that to me. I didn't want to. I knew enough, but he shifted toward me, and so I lowered my head and I listened.

I heard his weak, beating heart. I thought he had a month left. I was about to tell him, but he pawed me away, not wanting to know.

Follow the tracks, he said.

I left him. I crossed the field toward the platform. I was about to leave but changed my mind and headed into the train car, startling a rat who screamed and ran. I almost chased after the rat.

Instead, I brought back a tin of meat to the old dog. I did this a few times, leaving the tins in the garden beside the broken statue. Then I dragged the water bowl in and placed it so that it was under open sky.

I told him to stay inside as much as possible. I said I had seen a man pulling a cart a few days' journey from here, a man I did not like, a dangerous man, and if he ever heard a cart, to hide.

Before I left him there for good, the dog swung his head in my direction.

It was a wonderful way station, he said. Once upon a time.

THE CITY

I followed the tracks. I walked past the overturned train cars, past all the broken windows, and found a stretch of ground running parallel that was smooth enough to trot on.

I didn't like the open space. I didn't like that there was no shade in the daytime, but it also meant I could see far in all directions, too. I made sure to turn around on occasion even though the wind was on my back.

There was more of nothing. Silence. No movement, no flashes. Just the occasional distant airplanes above the mountain range and the engines of trucks too far to see, or for them to see me.

I scanned the ground for any shadows of birds overhead, but there were still no birds.

When I grew tired, I slowed to a walk. I found some more rainwater I sniffed before drinking. I approached rows of large craters in the earth and peered down at vehicles and tires and the rib cages of cows and smaller animals—coyotes, perhaps, foxes, some dogs.

I curled into a ball and tucked myself inside the curve of a cow's ribs that had gone white and soft from weather. I woke up and watched the ribs cast shadows on my paws and the earth.

When it grew dark, I climbed back out. The moonlight was again everywhere in the fields, and the mountains were hardly visible.

I pushed on.

I spent a day at a large, abandoned train station, where I found more water and where I hid under a bench as a massive truck stopped on a road, music blaring on its radio. I didn't move. I scanned the ground and followed the path of brown boots stepping through the empty doorframe and some men talking in English and scanning the lobby.

One of them wondered out loud if there was a train to someplace called Ohio, and another said that he wanted *to get the fuck out of here*—why did everything in this shit country smell horrible?

Because you're in it, bro, another person said.

Because you're in it, bro, I said to myself, wanting to remember that.

I heard more footsteps. Another man appeared inside the station, asking what was taking so long.

I caught a scent and went cold. A moment later, a dog appeared. He had big paws. He smelled me immediately, though he didn't pull on the lead.

He lowered his head to sniff, and that was when our eyes met.

He had black eyes. And large, pointed ears.

We stared at each other.

I breathed.

He breathed.

The dog with his head lowered at me and me facing him under the bench.

Then he nodded slightly and lifted his head so that all I could see were his legs as they all—him and the men—stepped across some papers and glass and rooted around behind the counters.

No money, someone called, and they left, the truck starting, the music blaring again.

I stayed there for another night, listening, hearing more trucks. The moon coming in. Loose paper flapping from small movements. I found another mouse to eat, and then to my surprise, a baby rabbit who had a broken leg.

I ate both fast and, with my belly full, I decided to return outside to the tracks I had been following. By now, I couldn't tell which direction the men and the dog had gone. If they were moving away from the city, it was possible that they would eventually find the old dog.

I wondered what would happen when they did. Maybe nothing at all. But I thought of going back.

Then, in the moonlight and the empty, silent dark, the land suddenly seemed even more vast. The feeling was heavy around me and made me sit, and I tilted my head up and kept smelling and listening to the vastness.

I thought of how much farther I had to go to get to the city. I knew I had to get to the city to get to the coast, but I didn't know how to find the coast from there. And how much farther after that to get home.

I was aware, with a new intensity, of my aloneness.

I whimpered a little, but I made it stop. I scratched my head with my paw, shook my body, hard, while above me a cloud flew across and the landscape grew brighter.

And it was then, in the direction of the city, toward the horizon farther along the tracks, that I saw a strange shape. It resembled another building of some kind. So I headed there, but as I got closer, I saw that it wasn't a building at all. It was a fighter jet. It had crashed so hard it had shoveled itself into the earth and was sticking out, one wing intact, pointing at the sky like a baby mountain that had yet to grow into an adult mountain.

I stopped to listen. I sniffed the perimeter. I climbed the jet until I could peer into the cockpit. The window had completely shattered; I didn't notice at first the remains of the pilot in the front seat until my nose grazed some strands of hair on the back of his skull.

I searched for a flag on him but couldn't find one. He was also missing his helmet. Someone had tried to take his jumpsuit off, probably years ago, and one skeletal arm was twisted and exposed.

I wasn't sure why, but the way he sat there leaning forward made me recall the way Jason once sat on a piano bench in an abandoned house, years ago.

And, recalling this, I licked the pilot's exposed arm.

I tasted the bone of him and the years of weather in the bone. I tasted something different that might have come from his home, wherever that was, and then I became aware of what I was doing, the licking, and I grew embarrassed and retreated.

I was about to jump down when I caught, behind him, near the floor, a bird's nest. The nest was empty, but I stayed up there on the jet for a while, staring down at the shape of it: the curve of the branches as they wound together, the circle that was balancing there behind the man in the dark.

I walked far enough until it was another morning and the tracks weren't broken anymore. They skirted a river—a river!—and I was about to cross over when I heard the tremble and metal of a cargo train approaching.

I was tired. I was thirsty. I knew I should move away, but I just wanted to cross over to the river. I got down low, waiting for it to pass.

I didn't think a car door would slide open.

But I heard the slide, and I was getting up to run away from the tracks, when a pair of hands reached down and scooped me up into the train car.

I flailed. Darkness. The ground shaking. I snapped the air with my teeth and growled and barked as someone clapped and cheered. All around me was the scent of horses, so at first I thought the shapes in the corner were animals, but I couldn't see. I raised my hackles in the dark as high as I could, and I lunged and barked, and I felt the same pair of hands run down my back. A voice spoke in this country's language, saying, Hey, hey, good guys, good guys, and he let me go, and I hurried to a corner and turned, growling loudly and baring my teeth.

I snapped the air. I kept hearing that voice say the same thing. I scanned the shapes silhouetted against the open door. I couldn't tell how many were there; I knew there were no animals here. Some people had their hands raised, but it was too dark inside to see much else.

If they all came for me at this moment, I'd be dead. But the more time passed, I felt no threat. Still, I kept scanning each body and set of hands, and I kept growling, staying low, but I didn't lunge.

My eyes adjusted better to the dark inside. I counted almost a dozen people of various ages in the corner opposite me. We were all inside a large car with some boxes against the wall. There was some loose straw on the ground.

Why in the world did you do that? I heard one in the back say.

I was trying to save him, another person said.

Save him from what? What do we need a dog for?

No one responded until someone else said, All God's creatures.

Amen, the first voice said.

Amen, everyone else echoed.

What do you know about creatures, I said.

Then everyone spoke all at once like: *He's lighter than he looks, I could pick him up with my hands. What happened to him? Look at his fur. Don't talk like that, you wouldn't want someone talking to you like that. I don't have fur. You know what I mean. I don't think he looks that bad. We could bring him to the orphanages. He might be good for the orphan children to see. It might bring a smile to their faces to see a dog. If we can fatten him up a bit. And give him a bath. He smells horrible. Can't we find a cuter one? When we get to the city, let's ask the first orphanage if they want him.*

I tested again to see if anyone could hear me speak: Excuse me, are we near the coast? The sea?

I stared. No response. I watched as they collectively pressed their hands together and said a prayer for the children they were about to visit.

When they were finished, they sang a song as the train moved smoothly across the land. The song sounded familiar to me. But it was difficult for me to remember human songs, to remember if I had heard them before.

Every time I heard a human singing it felt like I was hearing the song for the first time.

Maybe I was. Maybe every human had their own song they carried with them, like it was another heart, the way the men in my unit sang by themselves, wearing their headphones at night.

I never learned how to sing.

My mother used to tell me that we were land animals and that singing wasn't for us. We howled. We lumbered about and we barked and we shouted and we talked.

Singing was for the birds. And the sea animals that would on occasion appear near the coast from the far deep.

But once I heard two horses sing beautifully together, side by side on the ridge of a distant hill as we walked by on our way to a town. Only the dogs could hear them. It was better than any human I had ever heard. Better than the sea animals and the birds.

As the train car shook and the land sped past, I realized I was saving myself kilometers. As soon as I thought this, I felt the ache in my limbs from all the walking pulse through me, and I lowered myself down in that corner. I breathed and let the ache come strong at first, and then it dulled, and I rested and gazed out the open door as houses appeared. Or what was left of them: entire rooftops had slid down over stone walls and onto the streets.

I watched as a girl used an umbrella to lift a piece of large tile and peek under a fallen home.

I spotted a cat sitting on the street beside a toppled refrigerator, staring at us.

I lifted my nose and inhaled, sifting through the scents in the air, trying to figure out if I had passed through this area before—if we were approaching a city I had been to before, if there was a standing building that seemed familiar to me—but this was no place I had ever been.

Someone placed a cup of water in front of me. I drank it all. They gave me another cup. Then a hand appeared, flat, the palm holding a ball of rice, and I devoured it, licking the palm.

There was giggling. I wagged my tail. Another rice ball appeared, and I ate that, too. Someone else said to cut it out, that there wasn't enough food, but I went over to the closest body I could find and lay beside whoever it was, I couldn't tell, old or young, man or woman, and they ran their hand over my head and along my side and said that I was a good boy.

I wagged my tail again.

I leaned up to the hand.

I heard breathing. I smelled damp grass under fingernails and leaned against the bodies. Their calm limbs. A hand now pulling on my ears.

I thought, It's not so bad with them; it won't be so bad to stay with them for a while.

But just as I was about to fall asleep, someone said that after this visit to the city, they would have to figure out how to keep going inland to visit the rest of the orphanages. And that was when I knew they were heading in the opposite direction of the coast, that I couldn't follow them.

So I kept myself awake, facing the open door.

The smells changed. Charcoal. Batteries. Plastic. Landfill.

Rounding a bend, the train slowed. I leaned up to the hand again one more time.

And then, as they sang some more, I leapt off.

There wasn't much left of the city. Most of the buildings had fallen. The fallen buildings blocked off roads.

I spent the whole day roaming, staying close to whatever remained of walls.

In some open spaces, tents had popped up; in other areas, people had used the debris to build their own shelters. I also saw people living in whatever was left of the buildings. I could see those people asleep or crouched, washing their clothes, pissing into a bucket, or trying to boil water.

Eventually I found the river again. Crowded on both sides of the banks were rows and rows and rows of shanties. Endless shanties. It was like a new city had formed within the old one: some had metal rooftops; others, wood; many were painted different colors. Not all of them had doors. People had hung blankets or curtains instead, and on occasion I could see an arm sticking out and pushing the fabric aside or sliding the fabric shut.

There had once been a bridge connecting both sides of the riverbanks, but that was gone. Only the bridge's foundations remained, sticking up out of the ground, graffitied in blues and reds, in shapes I couldn't decipher.

(I forgot to say that I once heard a trainer at the base say that dogs couldn't really make out all the colors humans could see.

What a silly thing to believe.)

On the riverbank, some men were smoking cigarettes and lingering by a boat and a wooden raft. I watched as another man came up to one of them and offered food. I understood that it was payment to cross to the other side. The others watched the crossing. They seemed bored. And tired, like me. Their clothes hung loosely on them. They ignored me, too.

Yet I kept my eyes on them as I sniffed the water and drank. I paused, facing my reflection that had appeared there, clear in the sun.

I moved my ears a little and my reflection did the same.

Then water dripped down from my tongue and broke me apart.

I smelled them before I heard them. Three dogs. They came up behind me, near the top of the bank, and flanked me, one in the center, leading.

This is our side, the leader said.

I bowed to them, said that I was no threat.

They kept stepping down the bank. I bowed again and lay on my stomach and wagged my tail a little.

You have no business here, the leader said.

I'm just passing through, I said.

It doesn't seem like you're passing through, he said.

The men on the bank had now noticed the dogs approaching me, and they lit more cigarettes to watch.

I wagged my tail again and asked the dogs if they knew how far the coast was from here. That's all I wanted to know. And that I was leaving now.

I stood back up and stepped back into the water. I knew what was about to happen and breathed, ignoring my tiredness, watching their shoulders and legs.

I didn't want to fight dogs.

The left one lunged first, but I was faster and nipped him on the shoulder, once, hard.

I had to move faster than them now. And so as he backed up and away, I charged the leader. I ran up the bank and leapt and grabbed him by the throat and tackled him onto the slope, but then the third was on me, and I felt him bite into me, into my shoulder, and I bit the leader harder.

I heard the leader yelp, and his throat stiffened between my teeth. The one biting me bit harder, too, into my shoulders, and then it became a test of who would let go first.

I would not let go first.

The blood of the one I was on top of filled my mouth, and now I felt my own blood running down my front. And then I heard the second one, the one I had nipped, moving toward us.

And as I was about to pass out, I heard a crack, a loud yelp above me, and I let go. The dogs scampered away from me, all three of them, and dispersed up the bank, disappearing into the city.

I stood there panting, catching my breath.

Let me see how bad it is.

I turned to the voice and saw a man kneeling on one knee, holding a thick stick. He dropped the stick, and I let him come closer to me. He tapped around my wound; I winced.

I think it actually looks worse than it is, he said.

He ran his hand down my back. And then he mentioned that he was on the other side when he saw the dogs come up from behind me.

He was wearing a hat and had a bag over his shoulder. When he took off his hat to wipe his brow, I could see that he was a little older, or at least older than the men in my unit. He had some gray streaks in his hair. Wrinkles around his eyes. But he had broad shoulders and moved with confidence. Like the group on the cargo train, he spoke this country's language, though with an accent I couldn't place.

He stepped back toward the water, and I followed him. He was watching to see if I could walk. I could.

I've had worse, I said, but of course he didn't respond; he couldn't hear me speaking to him.

You should see the other guy, I added, which was something Jason used to say.

He wiped my wound with the water and then cupped some water with his hands, and I drank from them.

I haven't seen you before, he said. You're new. My name is Hong.

Hong.

I had learned over the years that some humans spoke over us, as though we couldn't be bothered to really listen or understand; others spoke to us as though we understood each other perfectly, as though whatever they said would be safe with us. Hong was the latter.

I watched intently as he opened his bag. He took out a knife and a small towel and cut the towel in half and tied it to make it longer. Then he wrapped it around my shoulder as tightly as he could.

There, he said, and stood. Come here.

He walked up and down the bank. I followed him. My shoulder had stiffened and swelled, but the towel was tight and was slowing the bleeding.

Good boy, he said, and his face softened, almost like a dog's, as Hong smiled. Good boy. There you go. You'll be all right.

Then he stroked my head, and I leaned up to his hand as he told me he had to get back to work but that he would be around at the clinic later that night.

Where's the clinic? I said, as he kept stroking my head.

Good boy, Hong said again, and then he walked back to the raft, stepped on, and I watched him cross back to the other side.

I didn't know where to go.

I stood by the river, panting less, but panting. I tried walking some more on my own. I felt the bruise and the soreness in my shoulder. I smelled my own blood and the blood of the other dog.

But the man named Hong was right. It wasn't so bad. I thought I would be better in a few days. But I needed someplace to rest.

Where did you learn to fight like that?

I turned to find another dog peering out from behind one of the stone squares of the bridge foundation. He was younger and smaller than I was. Thin, like the old dog, but shorter ears and a gray coat.

Like what? I said.

You weren't scared, he said. That whole time. You weren't scared.

I was scared, I said.

He didn't believe me. I told him he could come out, that I wasn't going to hurt him.

He came out shyly, and I let him sniff me. His nose hovered over one of my scars and then he licked the towel around my shoulder, tasting my blood.

You almost got one of them, he said.

They almost got me, I said.

Naw, he said. You had them.

He softened his brow and stuck out the tip of his tongue.

I asked if he had a name, and his eyes widened and he said eagerly, Yes! As of last year. Semeru. Semeru is my name.

I told him mine.

That's a strange name, he said.

So is yours, I said.

He shrugged. I wouldn't know, he said. That's just what the woman named me. She said the war was over, but she would still give me a name. I didn't know what she meant by that, but I have a name.

I stared at him curiously, and he looked away. I waited for him to go on, but he moved back to the dogs who had attacked me: All they do is fight. Those three. They're going to get killed one day.

I considered the size of him and asked if he was alone here.

He leaned down and stretched.

I said that it wasn't smart to be alone here.

Look who's talking, he said and snorted. Anyway, I'm strong.

He was getting more and more comfortable around me. He was light-footed and full of energy, but I could tell that the caution in him was there, in the way he carried himself and scampered about, unable to keep still. It was just no longer directed at me.

He asked again where I had learned to fight and if I could teach him, and I said maybe.

A cat appeared on the bank's ridge and snickered at us.

You got your ass kicked, the cat said.

Fuck you, cat! Semeru said.

Fuck you, dogs, the cat said and bounded away.

When we were alone again, Semeru said, Does it hurt?

A little, I said, and moved around some more by the river, feeling the cool water on my paws. I watched as another raft crossed over and two kids wearing paint on their faces splashed each other on the other side of the bank.

You're strong, like me, Semeru said, and he licked my face.

Particles of city buildings hovered in his breath.

I asked if there was a good place to rest. A safe place. A place for me to sleep. But not here.

The clinic, Semeru said, moving lightly around me in a half circle. We can go there. The guards don't ever bother us, they have enough to focus on. I haven't been there in a bit. I like to stay in different places every few days. I think it's better that way. But sometimes at the clinic, the man, Hong, he'll bring out food to us if he has any.

But it's still nice, even if he doesn't have food, Semeru added. There's a shed in the back. There's shade. There's grass.

I eyed Hong across the river, going from one shanty to another. I asked Semeru if the man was a doctor.

In the war, Semeru said. He was a doctor, yes.

Semeru told me that the woman Hong lived with was also a doctor. She was now a doctor at the clinic. He wasn't really a doctor anymore, but she still was. If you heard people mention a doctor in the city, it was probably her they were referring to.

Is she the woman who named you? I asked.

No, a different one, Semeru said. Though they all know one another. I think they all worked together during the war. I suppose they still do.

Semeru kept talking about Hong. He told me Hong did a lot of things: He helped at the clinic, and he went into the mountains to help the communities there. He also went around recording the population in the city, which was what he was doing at this moment. He was recording the people coming and going. Their names. If they were healthy or sick. What medicine they needed. And then he sent that information to somewhere else.

It was a way to keep track of the people here in the city, Semeru said. To figure out what medicine they needed more of. But it was also a way for people to find other people. Missing people. Displaced people. Family members.

Semeru paused. He said he wished they could do that for dogs. What was the word? he said.

I knew what it was. I said, A census.

Yes! That's it. A census for the dogs.

I asked whom he would find. If he could.

Too many, he said, briefly shutting his eyes.

You know a lot about this place, I said.

It's my city, he said.

Were you here? I asked. Through it all?

Yes, he said.

And then, after another pause: How long do you think it takes to destroy a city?

The way he said this, it sounded like the start of one of those jokes the men in my unit had shared with one another. Semeru drank some water from the river and sat to watch the kids playing on the other side. The paint on their faces had smeared.

The reflection of the sun kept breaking.

The strange thing is the destruction took longer than we thought, Semeru said. Or it seemed to. It just went on and on. The terrible noise. The bombs. The collapse. Just when you thought there was nothing left to destroy, it just went on. The collapse. The bombs. The smoke. The terrible noise.

The bomb noise?

No, he said.

He went silent. He lifted his paw and examined his dewclaw, which had chipped. He licked it and then scratched the top of his head with it and repeated the process. He resembled a cat.

Were you someplace where there were a lot of us?

I said, Not many, no.

Were you in one place?

I said, No.

My shoulder throbbed. The water on my coat was drying from the sun.

And then I asked Semeru if he had ever run into a dog named Fuji—she had blue eyes, a pale stripe on her chest, and a mole on her tongue.

He thought about it.

I'm sorry, he said. No. I don't think so. That's a funny name, too.

A thought I couldn't read flickered in his eyes. He licked his nose and said, Do you dream of the well?

I startled. What did you just say?

The well, he said. In the forest. For a long time, it was all I dreamed. Then I met another dog one day who dreamed the same thing and I thought it must be something we all dream. The well in the forest. Do you want to hear something strange?

Semeru looked down at his reflection.

I've never seen a well, he said. In person. I just know what it is because of the dream.

I tried to remember if I had ever seen one in this world, too.

What if it's not a well at all? I asked. How would we know what it is?

He paused to think about that, too.

I just know it is, Semeru said. I'm certain. It's like . . .

Faith, I said. It's faith.

Yes. Faith. What do you believe in?

I could spot Hong again, visiting more shanties and taking notes.

The coast, I said. I believe in getting to the coast. Have you ever seen the coast?

Semeru shook his head; I leaned closer to him.

In your time here, I said, have you heard anyone mention it?

Maybe, he said. Probably. People talk. Mostly about the river, though. Not about any coast. Why?

I told him it was my home, that I was trying to get home.

The woman who named me might know, Semeru said. She's from the mountains. She comes to the city on occasion. It depends on who is driving the truck. They come down to pick up any supplies that are available from the clinic. It's for people trying to start their lives up there in the mountains. Sometimes Hong will go with them. Like I said, they all know one another from the war.

Have you ever been to the mountains? I asked.

Semeru pointed his nose toward them in the far distance, beyond the city. He began to whine.

The mountains? No! Never! They bring rifles with them whenever they go. It's chaos up there. There's fighting going on up there. Not soldiers, not armies. Something else. Something worse than what goes on here. There's fighting here sometimes, sure. But not like up there. People who can't stop fighting each other. For land, for medicine, whatever. Hong came back once with his arm all wrapped up. But many, many people live up there. All over. All survivors. Like the woman. She's the best. She gave me a name.

Now it was Semeru who leaned in, closer to me.

Can I tell you a secret? he said. She can speak to me. The woman. She can hear me speaking to her and sometimes she can even hear my thoughts, and she responds, like you and me. We have real conversations . . . me and the woman . . .

He was too pleased with what he just said to notice my reaction.

I asked when the woman would be here next, and he said he never knew. But we would know when the supply truck arrived, if we stayed close to the clinic.

Is it worse? Semeru said. Where you're coming from? Worse than here?

I wasn't sure. I was too focused on the woman he had just mentioned.

A noise broke the air, and I tilted my head back, ears up. A small black dot was floating in the air above us. I recognized the noise and the mechanical movement.

Is that what I think it is? I asked.

Yes, Semeru said, and I thought of those boxes in the train car at the way station, and I thought of the first time Jason tried to fly one and how it crashed into a tree.

I thought of Brian's giant laughter shaking the leaves on the tree.

I asked Semeru if drones meant soldiers nearby, and Semeru stuck out the tip of his tongue.

No, he said. The soldiers patrol and try to keep order, but there aren't enough of them here for the entire city. You can spend days without seeing them. There are guards at the clinic, but they're mostly volunteers.

It's the children, Semeru said. The drones are being flown by children. They find them buried in the debris. The ones you can control with the wristband. Somehow the kids fix them up and they fly them all over or they try to sell them.

Semeru went on: I remember how terrified I was. The first time

I saw one. All those years ago. I didn't know what it was. I can't explain it, but I was more terrified of them than gunfire. They were everywhere. I thought they were coming to end the world.

I kept watching the black dot in the air. I wondered who was watching us. I wondered if drones had replaced the birds.

Children, Semeru said again, and sighed. He climbed the bank and waited for me on the ridge.

Well, come on, he said.

Semeru led me through a part of the city I hadn't explored. I was limping slightly, and he patiently slowed his gait to stay beside me. I was relieved to see that the few people we walked by didn't care enough to pay any attention to us. They were busy scavenging for things to place into their plastic buckets or were lying down on their makeshift beds inside the remnants of buildings, staring at their phones.

Eventually, we arrived at a small, one-story concrete building that was intact. There was a chain-link fence around the perimeter. The guards were posted at the front. It wasn't unlike the barracks except there was a crowd sitting outside in a line, waiting to get in.

Some of them noticed us but then returned to the waiting. A woman on a crutch walked out past the guards, and before anyone could do anything, a young man ran by her, grabbed the crutch, and vanished down a street.

No one tried to stop the young man—not the crowd, not the guards. It happened so fast the woman didn't have time to stop walking. She kept walking without her crutch, right by us, limping the way I was limping.

A little of my blood had seeped through the towel. Some pain had flared up, but I could manage. I just wanted to rest.

Semeru led me right through the gate past the guards. We walked around the back, to where there was a shed and a full water bowl. We took turns drinking and then we lay down together in the shade of the eaves.

The supply truck, he said. It usually comes in the early mornings.

I wanted to say something back, but lying in the shade, feeling the cool blades of grass against my body, my head suddenly felt very heavy. I recognized the familiar smells of the past years. The chemical smell and the medicine smell and the blood smell and the fear smell. I listened to the voices in the rooms inside the clinic. A dehydrated voice. A sick voice. The cry of someone who had just lost a leg from a building collapse.

I heard a couple enter the front and say that they had come from very far away and that they were searching for their children. They said they had been searching for their children for years. Then they began to scream when no one in the clinic knew who the children were.

I heard running. One of the guards rushing in. Shouting. The couple being dragged away as they kept screaming, asking why this useless place existed.

Later, the clattering of vials. The gathering of needles and pills. The softness of gauze being unwound, which was always like the sound of a kite's string being unwound.

I tried to remember the last time I had heard a kite as someone else, someone sick of waiting, tried to rush past the guards.

I heard chaos move into another chaos and then back again into moments of calm.

I listened to it all, and to Semeru breathing beside me, and I slept.

I didn't dream of the well this time. I dreamed of the man pulling the cart. He left the cart on a train platform, stepped across a tree line, and walked a path up toward the way station, calling for the old dog to *come here, good boy, come here.*

I woke as the dream slipped away from me. I tried to focus and listen as far as I could and reminded myself it was only a dream.

Semeru nudged me with his snout and told me to snap out of wherever I was. He had never left my side. I noticed the water bowl was full again, and rather than a towel, someone had wrapped my shoulder in a fresh bandage.

Semeru mentioned that Hong had come out in the morning and given me a shot and two stitches, even though he wasn't supposed to. The clinic would call it a waste, to treat a dog, so it had to be a secret. He heard Hong say that the stitches would eventually melt.

I didn't remember any of it. It surprised me that I didn't remember any of it, I must've been out cold. It had been a while since I hadn't woken because of someone, or something, nearby.

With his mouth, Semeru picked up some jerky Hong had also brought out. Semeru had saved half for me. I devoured it. I felt my mouth water after I swallowed it. I couldn't help myself, I searched the ground for some more. He watched me and asked if I could get up, and I got up.

I want to show you something, Semeru said.

We headed down a street. The moving woke me up. As I moved, I could tell I was already better today than the day before. I felt almost good. I was hardly limping. Probably it was the shot. And the food.

I thanked Semeru for the food as we walked, and he licked my face, smiling at what I said, and went on ahead a little.

We made two turns and then came upon some rubble and building debris and the shells of dark, rusted vehicles, long burned.

I could smell no sea where we were walking, only the river on occasion.

We passed a tall building without a wall, and for a brief moment, I saw the three dogs who had come after me on a high floor. I no longer sensed a threat in them. I could see the dried blood all over the leader, but he was moving all right. They ignored us, following the paths of scents across the floor.

Semeru slowed at an intersection, hugging a building, and I stood behind him, listening. I heard first the voice of the man who had lifted me up into the train car. He was approaching a few children who were taking turns flying a drone. The man told them that there was a place they could stay, that the building had been cleared and was safe. That they could sleep safely there and that there was also a teacher who was going to come to start a school for them. He said they could follow him, and he would take them there.

The children glanced at one another. Then they called the man a *perv* (a word the men in my unit sometimes called each other), told him to go fuck himself, and they ran away, shouting.

A moment later, I heard the animal. I peered around the corner and spotted a donkey in front of a cart that two men were filling with debris. It had probably been years since I had come upon a living donkey. Semeru approached first. The men ignored us and began to lift a large piece of stone onto the back of the cart.

Go away, the donkey said. Can't you see I'm working?

His voice delighted me. It was like a soft bellow. Like a whale song entering my chest.

Semeru stood under him and sniffed his stomach.

I approached. He kept still, ignoring me as I lifted my nose up to his mouth. I smelled a rotting tooth, hay, engine smoke, and an abandoned hive he had chewed on.

Have you heard when the woman might come? Semeru asked.

Who? the donkey said.

You know who, Semeru said. The woman from the mountains. The woman who gave me a name.

The donkey snorted. A name? What's in a name a human gives you? And why is it always you, dog, for crying out loud? Why is it always you pestering me? After all these years. You just want to be friends with everyone. Why? Let me tell you, friends are another thing to lose.

Meet my new friend, Semeru said.

But the donkey continued to ignore me. As the men kept loading the cart, I could hear a distant megaphone telling people to move aside, and I heard the voices of those children earlier, climbing something.

I stepped back a little from the donkey. I asked him if he had been here the whole time. And whether he knew if there was a coast nearby. The sea.

I watched his ears twitch as, finally, the donkey peered down. I caught the smell of a hive again, his round, damp eyes moving across my body and the bandage on my shoulder.

What happened to you? he said.

Semeru, about to speak, lowered his head.

Never mind, the donkey said. His voice grew softer now as he looked me over one more time and said no to my first question: He hadn't been here in the city the whole time. He had come from a faraway village that no longer existed.

I waited for him to go on, but he didn't.

Another stone thudded onto the cart.

And the coast? I said. Do you know if the coast is nearby?

That's where he's trying to go, Semeru said.

Shut up, dog, we're having a conversation here, the donkey said.

I heard the megaphone again, a voice moving farther away.

It's where I'm trying to go, I said.

The donkey raised an eyebrow. Let me think, he said.

He lifted his front hoof and kicked the ground a little. And then he said that he met a seabird once. That the bird had flown in from the coast. But it was so many seasons ago, it was possible it was just a dream.

An enormous bird, the donkey said. I've never seen anything like it. I think maybe it was a dream. She terrified me.

I asked him to describe the bird, but he couldn't remember so well anymore.

Like a dream, he said again.

From behind the cart, someone shouted at someone else.

Do you believe in spirits? the donkey said.

Only the bad ones, I said, and the donkey fluttered his lips.

Do you dream of the well? Semeru asked the donkey.

Shut up, dog, the donkey said, and moved his head closer to me. I haven't seen birds in a long time. But if you see them, ask them. Ask the birds. They'll know about the coast. The sea.

Or ask the woman, Semeru said.

The donkey sighed and shook his head. I thought he was going to tell Semeru to shut up again, but he said, Not today, dog. Maybe tomorrow. Or the day after. You should stay away from her. And whatever you do, don't go with her. It's dangerous. What they're doing up in the mountains.

What are they doing up there? I said.

I told you what they're doing up there, Semeru said, and pushed me with his snout.

They try to help the people up there, the donkey said. That woman and her friends. In the mountain villages that survived. But most times what they bring up is something other people want. Greedy people. Or desperate people who need help but got so used to fighting that they just keep fighting and taking. I think it's madness up there . . .

But now that I think about it, the donkey said. It's madness down here, too, no? These two dumb idiots behind me think that they can sell the garbage they're loading on the truck. And I bet someone else tonight will rob them, convinced it's something they can sell, and I'll play silent and dumb and hope I'll be spared and be used by someone else. What can we do? We live here, too.

One of the men who had been loading the cart appeared and began to yell: Hey, you lazy, stupid animal! Come on! Let's go!

The man hit the donkey with the shovel.

The donkey brayed loudly, cursing, jerking his head, and both men tried to kick me aside as the cart moved forward. I stepped back, growling. Semeru growled, too, but the men didn't care, they laughed at us as they kept the shovel raised.

Walking away, the donkey went on: Do you want to know what scares me the most? Truthfully, it's not the bombs. Or the gunfire. Or buildings falling. Or the fires. Or even thieves or bandits or what goes on in those mountains.

He started to go a little faster down the street as the men kept shouting at him.

What scares me the most, he called back, is that I could be eaten. That when there's no food left, I'll be butchered and eaten. By assholes like these two. And then maybe the leftovers to dogs like you, no? So I think: as long as I do this work, I won't get eaten. That's what I think.

I would never eat a donkey, Semeru whispered to me.

The men hit the donkey again.

Don't go to the mountains, the donkey shouted, pulling the cart farther and farther down the street.

I wanted to keep walking, to see how the walking felt.

We went the opposite direction, over the debris, and turned the block to find another damaged building. I could see that it had once been a parking garage, underground, though those floors were no longer accessible. The ramp going down had caved in. I could smell the rubber of the car tires down there, the rusted metal of the cars themselves, some old skeletons.

The same cat from the river crossed our path quickly and vanished into a space, and I listened with some envy the way he headed down the floors to explore.

During the war, I always felt relief when I crossed paths with a living cat. It was because they appeared in unexpected places. High up in a tree or on the slope of a roof. Balancing themselves on a fence post. In the arms of a corpse in a ditch.

I liked the way they brought me out of the landscape, briefly, into a new place—a new level to see the world we were traversing.

The ramp heading up to the higher floors of the building hadn't collapsed. Semeru and I climbed up to the second floor. It was all open space with the painted parking lines all over the ground. But instead of cars, multiple tents had been set up, a few per parking space.

A tall girl selling SIM cards and phones rushed toward us, petted us, and took out a granola bar from her coat pocket. Even though it wasn't raining, she was wearing a raincoat—I caught the swish-sound of it as she gave us each a bite of the granola bar. We sat in front of her, both of us, and she seemed hypnotized by this, our sitting, and so we kept sitting, waiting for more food, wagging our tails across the concrete lot until Semeru said, This is ridiculous. And that made me bark once with laughter, so I got up and left.

He said, Wait!, and followed after me.

I returned to the street. In Semeru's mouth was a piece of rope he had found in the debris, and he asked if I wanted to play. I grabbed the other end and pulled as he pulled, and we played tug in the street until I felt it in my shoulder and let go.

He said, I'm sorry, was that all right?

And I said, Yes, you're strong, and he was pleased.

I told you I'm strong, he said.

Another drone appeared overhead.

Fuck you, drone, Semeru said, and barked.

He gripped the rope with his mouth and bounced around me.

Later in the day, we returned to the river, to the shanties. I could smell Hong here. We must have just missed him.

Semeru entered the river where people were wading in to wash their clothes or just to stay cool from the heat. A man yelled at Semeru to stop splashing, and Semeru hopped back out. He was still carrying the rope, water dripping from the ends.

The effect of the shot was wearing off, but I felt good. The sutures felt familiar—like the ones that used to be on various parts of my body—and the familiarity felt good. Sutures meant I would heal, that I would get better.

We walked the paths of the shanties, sniffing for food. We heard people talking to each other or pleasuring themselves or each other or crying.

In one shanty, we sensed someone inside, but there was no breathing.

We stopped. We both sat and stared at the open, dark space, and Semeru shook his head and said, No way.

But I took a step forward and stepped in all the way. I smelled the old woman lying on the floor on her back with her hands clasped together. Her eyes and her mouth were open.

I smelled her wrist and the cave of her throat and the city dust and the river and the skin particles of other humans embedded in her thousand wrinkles.

I watched an ant climb over her teeth. And another one. I leaned forward and focused on the legs and antennas, as one of the ants stood to inspect me, almost grazing my whiskers.

I admired ants. Ants were forever.

I smelled all over until I found an open bag of potato chips in a corner that I carried out.

We found a quiet place to eat. I ripped open the bag wider and ate one chip, and Semeru ate one, and we took turns that way. After, Semeru chewed on the rope again, and I took the other end, and we played for a little while as we walked.

That night, I woke up to the moonlight on the low, wide window like a framed painting.

We had returned to the shed behind the clinic. Semeru was asleep on me, his head hooked over my back. His head rose and fell as I breathed calmly and faced the window: behind the glass, Hong was lying on the floor on his side beside the doctor, who was also lying on her side with her back facing him.

They were sucking on liquid energy packs and watching something silently on a phone that she held lengthwise. The screen illuminated their faces. Their eyes flashed.

I never learned why, but we could never see what was on those phone screens, even when on occasion a man in our unit would lower their phone and show something to us dogs. The screen was just a blur of flashes and colors to us, bothering our eyes.

Tonight, here, those days suddenly felt like a very long time ago. Like they were being carried away by a kite. A great bird. It occurred to me that I had completely lost track of how many days had passed since I had walked away from the base. Tonight, here, that day, too, felt like a very long time ago.

Tonight, here, every day except today felt like a long time ago.

I stretched quietly, feeling the cool night grass and Semeru on me. I felt the tension in my shoulder that was healing. I breathed and knew I had the strength to bolt right now if I needed to.

The old dog came to me again. I lifted my ears forward and shut my eyes and tried to float as far as I could out of the city, over the shantytowns by the river and the small fires and voices and the train tracks. Then, with my eyes still tightly shut, I floated back through the rooms of the clinic, listening to the patients as they appeared in and out of my mind until I located Hong and the doctor lying together in their room near the window.

Their phone battery had died. The doctor put the phone away and began to talk. She talked about the next shipments of medicine and aid that never arrived from the West. She was worried the shipments would never arrive. What was the point of them being here in this city if there was nothing they could use to help people?

We can't help if there is no help, she said.

Hearing them now, I could tell she was younger than he was. Healthy. Tired, but alert. Alert to Hong as he stroked her wrist and told her about a dog—me—he had met the other day. That he had saved me while I was being attacked and how, when he went up to me to tend to the wound, he was able to see the scars all over my body.

Shrapnel, he said. I think they were from shrapnel.

You're telling me, she said, that's the first dog you've encountered here with shrapnel scars?

No, he said. Of course not. It was just . . .

She waited for him to go on.

He was different, Hong said. He didn't seem terrified. He wasn't aggressive. It was like he knew things.

You suddenly know everything about dogs, she said.

Someone worked fast, he said. And got whatever went through his body out.

Probably not all the pieces, she said.

He survived, Hong said.

Yes.

They grew silent; she pressed her back up against his chest. His arms moved over her.

If the dog survived, Hong said, we'll survive. I guess that's what I'm trying to say. If he survived, we will survive. Every day this dog lives, we live.

Maybe he's no longer alive, the doctor said.

Actually, he said. I think he's outside our window right now.

Really? she said, but didn't get up, just stayed where she was.

Hong, she said. Promise me: I don't ever, ever, ever want a dog.

Which made him laugh.

He's not ours, Hong said. Don't worry.

What else?

What do you mean?

Tell me more about your day, she said. We haven't talked all day. Tell me a story. To help me sleep.

He held her and thought about it. He said today he met a man who asked if he was a believer of God.

Oh God, she said.

He said it was because some missionaries helping with the orphanages across the country had passed through, handing out water and snacks in the shantytowns. But this man kept talking. He was from a different country—far, far north. He had come down here years before the war. He said that soldiers came one night into his home village and they rounded up the men who believed in God. They tied the men's wrists together and led them up the mountain. They were going to be executed, you see, for believing in God . . .

He was just a boy then, and the men had taken his father. He was under the floor of the house with his sister, in the space where they shat, and their mother was on the main floor praying and praying so hard she clawed the floor until she ripped off her fingernails. And while his mother was doing this, the boy's father was up on a trail with his hands tied, the very last one in that line of men about to be executed. The guard beside him was only a boy, too. The guard was bored. Or exhausted. Both. He left the back to check on the guards up front. And that was when his father leapt down the mountain.

He just leapt? the doctor said.

Without thinking, Hong said. In an instant. And soon after, his wife, still praying, heard a noise. She opened her eyes to see her husband there, back to her, praise God, and they all escaped their country that night, heading south. They would spend weeks on boats, trains, roads, paying the people whom they needed to pay to cross the borders, and they kept going. And all the while they prayed. They just prayed . . .

When the war started here, when the fighter jets finally came over the field where their new house was—the house they had settled into after escaping their own country—you know what the parents did? They stopped to pray. It was like a switch. Like something they couldn't control. Like it was something else that was controlling them. They got on their knees in the middle of the field in the grass and let go of their children and prayed. And that was the last the man saw of them: his parents kneeling in the grass as their bodies evaporated ten yards behind him.

Hong cleared his throat. He rubbed his eyes and tucked the doctor's hair behind her ear.

That's what I heard today, Hong said. And that I should never stop moving. And then the man punched the wall and told me to put that in my stupid fucking census.

Hong shifted beside her and wrapped his arms around her more tightly.

One day, when I'm mad at you, the doctor said, I'll tell you to put that in your fucking census.

And punch a wall, Hong said.

The doctor made a fist and stabbed the air.

Maybe the man is right, Hong said. Maybe what I'm doing to help the city is stupid. Maybe I should help here more. Maybe I should go up to the mountains more.

Yes, she said. Yes. Help here. Be with me. But don't go to the mountains. Please. Don't go up there anymore. When the truck comes tomorrow, you don't have to go. You can just give them the supplies.

We owe her, Hong said. Think of how many times she helped us during the war. She got us more medicine. She went out there and kept going out there to find the supplies that never made it to us. That was her.

War's over, the doctor said.

Not up there, Hong said.

They shot at you last time. It's getting worse.

I can shoot back, he said. Don't you remember that I'm . . . how do you say it in English? A crack shot?

You're being a child, Hong. A child. Put that in your fucking census.

I want to help, he said. I can teach those people living up there how to administer medicine. What to do. What is what. Easy stuff. I won't be gone long. I never am. Besides, I wouldn't mind a change.

You mean, a change from me, she said.

Shut up.

You're already exactly what that man advised, she said. You never stop moving. Like at the hospital. You were the one always on your feet, moving through the wards, all night. The other doctors and the officers there called you the somnambulist. Did you know that?

I was afraid to go to sleep! he said.

You still are, she said.

Yes, he said. I still am.

She leaned up to kiss his chin.

If the dog survived, you will survive, she said.

That's the attitude, he said, kissing her back on the cheek. Do you know who that man reminded me of? The one who told me about his praying parents and who punched the wall today?

Who did he remind you of?

Do you remember the Greek?

The Greek?

The one who survived in that valley and walked into the hospital that winter. He walked for days through the fighting and the snow. He had lost everyone he had been fighting alongside. I think he was out of his mind. Totally lost it. He had no idea what he was doing, so he just kept walking through the snow. And bleeding.

The Greek brigade, she said. I remember now. Achilles. His name was Achilles. Like the warrior in the poem.

Yes.

We took care of him. And then one day we were posted elsewhere. We never saw him again.

Yes.

I wonder what happened to Achilles, she said.

Maybe someone named Paris got him with an arrow, Hong said.

If only we were treating arrow wounds, she said.

I don't know, Hong said. I think those were pretty bad, too.

So this is your story? she asked. About the Greek?

No, Hong said. One night, I sat with him. Achilles.

You did?

Yes, Hong said. In the ward. I couldn't sleep, of course. So I lit a candle and held it and sat by his cot. I didn't know his language; he didn't know mine. But I could tell, in his eyes, he wanted me to talk. I think it made him feel more . . . anchored. Shielded. To hear me talking. To see that tent of candlelight I was holding. It was a way to erase the screaming and the guns and the weeping and the running. God, the wards. They were like cities.

Or maybe the talking and the candlelight was actually for you, she said. To anchor you. To shield you. From everything else.

He paused. Yes, maybe.

Go on, she said. The Greek.

My father used to tell me fables, he said. Do you remember those? From when we were children.

I don't think I do, she said.

There are so many of them. Hundreds and hundreds of them. Centuries old. But that night, beside Achilles, I remembered one of the war ones, so I told it to Achilles.

I bet that cheered him right up, she said.

He didn't understand a word of it!

She grinned. Well? she said.

Hong cleared his throat again. A small shadow entered the frame of moonlight on the far wall and vanished.

Hong said, Once upon a time, on a hilltop, there was a tree. A big, old, tall tree. And one night a bird flew by, and the tree said to the bird, Hurry! Come be with me and my shadow, I think the war is about to begin. So the bird flew back to the tree and waited on a branch in the tree's shadow for the war . . .

But the war didn't come. A fox did, however, appearing on the slope, and the bird said to the fox, Come be with us, I think the war is about the begin! So the fox sat against the trunk of the tree in the tree's shadow and waited for the war . . .

But the war didn't come. The moon did, however, its light flooding the city and the distant hills as it approached the tree. And the tree said, Don't worry, bird and fox, you're safe here with me and my shadow. The moon can't reach you if you're with me . . .

And together, both the bird and the fox said, Tree, why should we be afraid of the moon? Look at how beautiful it is. Look at how grand and bright and peaceful it is. It's never done anything to us but shown us the way.

So then leave, said the shadow of the tree, speaking for the first time and shrinking as the moonlight quickly began to surround them all.

But they didn't leave, Hong said. Neither the bird nor the fox.

He stopped. The doctor had fallen asleep in his arms minutes before, but he was noticing only now.

Hong tucked her hair behind her ear again. Quietly he slid out from under her and moved closer to the window.

I couldn't tell if he could see me and Semeru by the shed.

I could hear Hong breathing loudly. I stayed motionless and watched as his body began to shake. I watched him lift his hands and cover his face as his body shook like a tree in the wind, and he wept.

And then the shaking ended. He stepped away from the window, vanishing from us, and then there was only Semeru asleep beside me and the night.

Once, at a field hospital, I overheard a medic who was assigned to us saying to the men in my team that if we were lucky, we would probably live ten years. All of us dogs in the war. Not much more than that after what we had gone through. He meant not only the wounds but what the noises—the explosions, the gunfire, the grenades, the shelling, the fighter jets, the tanks—what all of that did to our brains. He showed Jason and Brian and the others gathered around something on his phone I couldn't see. I was three years old then. He was giving all the dogs a checkup.

The war will be over in two, so it doesn't matter, I heard a man in our unit say, and then laughter.

And then the doctor said, Your brains, too.

No one responded to that. They gathered us up, and we went back to work.

Wake up.

I woke up. Semeru was nosing me. I forgot where I was. I thought he was someone else. I showed him my belly and stretched, and he nosed me there, and then I smelled him and remembered.

It's time, Semeru said.

Time?

The truck's in the city. It's arriving. Let's see.

I got up. I shook myself awake and pissed and followed him.

I was even better today than I was yesterday. I felt that I could go faster than Semeru, but I let him lead.

The sun was dim. It began to rain. Lightly. The droplets hit our coats and slid down. It cooled the air. Across a road, a man pushed out a bowl from an open tent.

We headed to the other side of the clinic, to what must have once been a market square. One of the children I had heard yesterday was sitting on top of a dirt mound, watching as other dogs appeared from different parts of the city, all of us ignoring one another and focused on the pickup truck that was pulling into the square.

The supply truck! Semeru said.

I sat and went still. I listened as dogs whined and whimpered as a man I had never seen before got out, stepped up onto the truck bed, and began to toss us cut-up chicken meat, telling us to keep calm, that we would all get some.

Semeru hurried over, but I stayed back. I remained sitting. I scanned the whole area to see if there was a woman I had missed, but no other human was there. I called to Semeru to ask. He returned with a piece of chicken for me and said the woman didn't come today.

The rain stayed light as Hong came out with a rifle and two large bags over each shoulder and slid the bags into the truck bed.

Before he could walk around to the front, I bolted and jumped onto the bed. I sat leaning my weight against the two bags and stared hard at him.

Hong stared back.

A sound like a drum cut the air, and I turned to see Semeru sitting beside me on the bed. I told him to get off, but Semeru neither moved nor spoke as he stared at Hong the way I had been staring at Hong.

I growled, only to Semeru, and he growled back. He told me he wasn't leaving my side.

I'm strong, he said.

You must be kidding me, Hong said.

Strays? the driver said, appearing from the front.

Chewing on a toothpick, the man took off his hat and put it on again.

I'm sorry, Hong said. I'll get them out.

Friendly? the driver said.

Very, Hong said.

Let them come, the driver said. Might cheer the kids up. Also, between us, it might not be bad. To be seen with dogs. Might make someone think twice before bothering us. Especially one that looks like that one over there.

The man pointed at me. And then he said, Anyway, she'll know what to do with them.

Hong grabbed my scruff, leaned close to me, and shook me gently.

You're trouble, he said, and I licked his mouth that tasted like sleep and bad water and what must have been the doctor's neck.

Hong quickly replaced the bandage on my shoulder with a clean one. Then he said to the two of us, Don't fall, and he jumped down.

Semeru was panting, excited. We sat beside each other, staring out as the truck started.

The rain continued to fall softly. It fell on the dogs beginning to disperse and a cat waiting for any pieces of chicken left behind; and the child on the mound, knees to her chest, watching the cat; and against a window behind which appeared the doctor, putting on her coat and waving to Hong as we left.

THE MOUNTAINS

I used to sleep under Jason's cot, in those times when there was a cot to sleep on. I liked the den of it. His hand falling down as he dreamed. His hand that smelled of gunpowder and metal and the gum he kept chewing all day. Sometimes, he stuck the chewing gum under the rim of his helmet so that he could save it to chew later. Sometimes, it fell and I picked it up for him and carried it in my mouth and later returned it to his hand as he slept.

I liked staring at the lines on his palms. That private map. I liked his irritation when I licked his hand as he slept, the way he would softly bat my face like we were playing a game while he was still in some dream.

I forgot to say that Jason wasn't born in this country, but his parents were.

And that he was steady with those wide hands because, he used to tell me, of the piano. Then he would wiggle his fingers in the air, as though I knew what a piano was.

And then one day I did know. Because, one day, we stayed in an abandoned house in a nearly abandoned town where there was a piano. Which he never once played, only sat in front of for a long time, bent over and staring. This was not long before we were granted furlough. Not long before Fuji disappeared.

She had been recovering from a graze from a bullet on her hind leg. The day we arrived, we had stumbled upon two enemy soldiers who had either gotten separated from their unit or were running away—one of them had fired upon us from a second-floor window, and I saw Fuji go down. Jason gave the command, and I charged. I leapt through a shattered first-floor window, climbed the steps, got ahold of the one carrying the rifle, dragged him down, and went for his throat. Just enough time to surprise and distract the other one as a man in my unit fired well above me.

Fuji would recover quickly. I remembered an old man from the town appearing in the quiet, not wearing shoes, and leading us to a house. How a house, because it was rare, made the men loosen their shoulders, made it okay for them to be apart from one another, in separate rooms or floors, and how no one objected to me staying by Fuji's side after she was patched up.

We found a spot in a room underneath a piano bench—another den for us—where we slipped in and out of sleep and woke to the noise of Jason sitting above us.

We had come here because we had smelled the dog, long dead, that no one had touched. Or Fuji had smelled the dog and wanted to be with her, and I had followed.

The dog was on the floor across from us. My guess was that the owners had left her here when they fled.

I had by then lost count of how many animal carcasses I had encountered.

This one had long golden fur and was lying on her side, the top half of her body in sunlight, the bottom in shadow.

Her eyes were entirely gone and I was grateful for that, that I didn't have to look at her eyes.

Brian had fallen asleep in another room. I could hear the footsteps of the others roaming the house, checking the other rooms.

Fuji let me smell the wound on her hind leg that was healing under the bandage. I pawed Fuji's face once to try to get her to stop staring at the dog. Fuji had gone up to her, inhaled, and come to me without a word or noise.

She was lying with her snout on her paws in a way that reminded me of the first time I had seen her in the back of Soojin's truck. I had not thought about that in a while.

Lying there under the piano bench, the old man outside collecting pieces of a beam for us for a fire, I thought about that day. I thought about Fuji when she was that young and frightened and about how I had once been that young and frightened, too. I thought about how over the years she was no longer frightened, but that some days she charged and fought like she was trying to get back to a time when she was frightened.

I thought and waited for Jason to do something about the dead dog. He had stepped over her to get to the piano but hadn't turned around again. He just leaned forward, above us, and we listened to his breathing and smelled the rottenness in the room that wasn't strong but did linger in the air, in the matted fur and the carpet, and I thought maybe he was trying to speak to the piano the way I often tried to speak to him.

As the war went on, Jason talked to me less. Only commands, or the occasional muttering as he exited a dream, his fingers gripping my scruff like a handle.

But that day in that room, as we waited to see if he would do something about the dog, he gazed out the window and said out loud and clearly, This was the town where my mother was born.

Fuji lifted her ears. I wasn't sure if he was talking to us or talking to himself. We would spend two nights in this house, clearing the town of any explosives, and then move out the next day to clear a road. We would leave the dog where she lay.

Jason kept talking. It's my first time here, he said.

And then he said it was the second time the town had been destroyed. That when his mother left, they were trying to rebuild the country because of the previous war.

Decades ago, he said. Look at where it got them.

I was listening, but I was also staring at the carcass. I thought the head had trembled. I glanced at Fuji, who had noticed it, too, and we both went low and waited.

This really happened: a butterfly appeared, climbing out of the dog's empty eye socket.

The butterfly was the color Fuji's eyes had once been, and it had black dots all over. It climbed out and balanced itself there, on the edge of the eye socket, like it had just come out of a tunnel and was seeing the world for the first time.

Hey! I said, trying to get it to speak to us. *Hey.*

When it didn't respond, I growled quietly, enough for Jason to turn around.

Holy shit, he said, and took out his phone.

But he didn't take a photo. He just stared at the butterfly and dropped his other hand past the seat of the bench to our eye level. Fuji moved her face away, shutting her eyes. And as Jason's hand swung like a pendulum in front of us, the old man came inside with a bundle of wood, and the butterfly climbed back down into the dog.

Heading up into the mountains, I wondered if there might come a time when I would lose the memory of that day—the clarity and the stillness of it—and how I would feel about that. How I would feel if one day I stopped carrying certain things in my head, so many of the things I kept returning to in my head—the farm, Fuji, the birds, a valley floor (and other things I hadn't yet talked about)—and whether this meant I had managed to go far enough away, into a time when all of this was old. Which would also mean a time when I was old, older.

Did I feel older?

I was now halfway through my life, according to what a doctor once said, years ago.

I carried that, too.

The road became more rough and narrow. Semeru kept trying to hide the fact that he was nervous about heading into the mountains and nervous about riding in the back of a pickup truck. Every time we sped over a bump, he held his breath and shifted closer to me.

What are you thinking about? he said.

I rested my head and a paw on his back to calm and steady him.

A piano, I said.

What's a piano? he said. Are they dangerous?

I don't know, I said.

Which was true. I didn't know if they were dangerous.

Are you mad at me? Semeru said. For coming along?

Yes, I said.

It's a strange way of showing that you're mad, he said.

I was still on top of him. The air rumbled and we watched the clouds and the hint of dark branches like an old woman's hair.

I saw no birds. The rain had stopped.

We traveled all morning and afternoon. For hours and hours, pausing only for the driver to pour gas into the tank. Daylight shifted as we kept heading up. Levels of air and moisture. Levels of the color green. We climbed and turned. The road changed from paved to dirt and then to almost no road at all as we entered the thickest forest I had seen since my first months in the war.

Like the city, I had never been to these mountains before.

We slowed. We passed a cluster of fallen trees in a clearing that formed a giant X in the air, and in the crux of it hung another fighter jet.

Just beyond were the remnants of a village. I caught a spot of color on the ground near a door, maybe a towel or a bucket.

The trees seemed to grow thicker and denser as we drove.

It was now late afternoon. Thin sunlight slipped down. Hong and the driver hardly spoke. On occasion, Hong turned around to check on us through the back window, tapping a knuckle against the glass and giving us the thumbs-up.

That was what he was doing when the truck rounded a bend on the mountain road and braked suddenly. Semeru and I slid forward toward the back window, and Hong jerked toward the dashboard.

A pile of stout logs was blocking the way.

I heard the driver say, Shit, that wasn't here before.

I watched as he grabbed the rifle between him and Hong.

I heard the first shot before it struck the windshield.

The windshield splintered, the bullet passing through it between the driver and Hong, and then back out between me and Semeru.

Hong ducked forward as another bullet barely missed us, this time shattering a side window.

The driver screamed. He dropped the rifle. He cried, I can't do this anymore, and he opened his door and stumbled into the woods, bolting toward the village we had passed.

Hong grabbed the rifle and began to fire out the open door into the trees.

I told Semeru to stay low. I waited to hear one more shot from the woods and then jumped down, rushing to the front where the first shot occurred, which had been the closest to us.

The person firing was standing behind a tree. He was short and stout like the logs, and he didn't hear me coming.

He swiveled around to fire again at the front of the truck, lowered his weapon slightly in surprise at seeing me, so I lunged at his face. My jaw locked around his cheekbones and nose, and as he fell, I bit down as hard as I could. I heard the shock and the pain, the sound shooting into my throat as I heard his bones break, and I tasted him, and I felt his face fold flat in my jaw.

Then I went for his throat and ripped it open. His body trembled as I swiveled around and ran back.

Hong was outside the truck. He was aiming at the trees to the side and checking the truck bed. The back window was shattered.

Semeru! I called.

I rushed over and jumped onto the bed. Semeru was crouched in the corner. I smelled him for wounds, but he was all right. I licked his face, smearing a little of the man's blood on his nose, but Semeru didn't lick back.

I smelled Hong, but he was all right, too.

Fucking coward, Hong said. He was cursing the driver.

I almost had him, Hong said, meaning the second shooter.

He then stared curiously down at me, at the blood on my mouth and my panting, was about to say something, but hesitated.

Thank you, he said, and ran a hand over my head.

I noticed a bag of medicine was missing. Hong took the other bag, slipped it over his shoulder and said, Come on, and I said, Come on, to Semeru, who shook his body and jumped down as I jumped down.

I didn't do anything, Semeru said. When the man came and got the bag.

Good, I said. Don't do anything. Hide and stay low.

He didn't even notice me, Semeru said. It was like I wasn't even there. He just fired into the window and grabbed a bag.

Good, I said.

I watched Hong trying to decide which way to go. I told him, Don't go to the village, that's where they'll think you'll have gone.

But of course he didn't hear me. He took a step toward the village. I was about to grab his pant leg, when he turned around again, changing his mind.

He checked his rifle, and we entered the forest, leaving the road, and continued farther into the mountains.

It wasn't until we were walking that I noticed I had lost a tooth. That had never happened to me before. It didn't hurt, but I pressed the tip of my tongue against the space, and my own blood leaked out a little as we hurried.

The later afternoon turned later; it warmed and cooled. Sweat darkened Hong's shirt. He was carrying the remaining bag on one shoulder, and the rifle was strapped over the other.

For every noise we heard, Hong made us stop, even though it was nothing. No one was following us yet. Hong kept checking his phone. I knew he didn't have service because he had tried to make a call earlier, but he was using the map. He said to himself, I think the village we were supposed to go to must be nearby. Where is it?

I checked on Semeru. He was panting but seemed all right. I told him to keep listening, ears up, and he did, walking alongside me.

I'm sorry, Semeru said, and I told him to shut up, that he did great.

I licked the space in my mouth where the tooth had been. A little more of my own blood.

Up ahead in the distance, beyond the trees, appeared a small house. A cabin. The roof had crumbled. Only a part of its chimney remained. The front door was closed.

Hong approached from one side. Semeru followed me as I flanked the other side. We rounded the house and entered a clearing in the back.

Etna, Semeru said. Look.

He had stopped. I followed his gaze.

Near a tree line stood a stone well.

I turned to see Hong peering into the back of the abandoned house through a hollow window frame. I turned back, but Semeru had already rushed to the well, sniffing eagerly around the perimeter of it. Then he stood on his hind legs and peered down, wagging his tail.

I joined him. I stood up, balancing my front paws on the rim. I peered down. I inhaled deeply.

Do you see anything? Semeru asked.

I saw nothing. But I smelled far water. Earth water. Ancient water.

My head began to hurt. My eyes got blurry. It was like I was being held and wrapped in cobwebs. The air vibrated; the daylight and the stones around me got brighter.

I growled quietly, got off the well, and spun around.

A woman was walking toward me, Hong following behind. She was carrying a medicine bag and her own rifle.

Then Semeru saw her, too, and barked once, and ran to her, crossing the clearing. The woman got down on one knee and greeted Semeru.

While she was petting him, she looked over at me, and I approached, and she said, only to me: *Etna, You've gotten old.*

So have you, I said.

I nudged her with my snout, smelling the mountains on her, smelling her neck, and I stood and placed my front paws on her shoulders, leaning on her, and Soojin ran her hands over my paws and legs.

She chuckled and said, Someone worked on their paw sensitivity, I see, and then she shut her eyes and lifted her chin to be licked.

In truth, I remembered she was still young, but staring at her now I could detect the years on her face and her shoulders: she had grown thin, and when she lowered herself onto her knee earlier, she hesitated slightly. But her long hair was in the braid I remembered. She had a thin scarf wrapped around her head, too, and around her wrist was the same drone device that the children had been using in the city.

So it's really you, I said. You're known. In the city.

It's me.

Is that the bag from the truck? I asked.

Soojin patted the bag. I got it back, she said. But I don't know if I got the man. I saw him run off. Maybe I clipped him. I was waiting for the delivery when I heard the gunfire and ran in your direction. I saw the man with the bag running through the forest and fired.

The driver, I said. He fled.

Sometimes people do, she said.

I licked some blood from my lips.

Are you talking to them? Hong asked, and Soojin nodded.

Ask him how he did that, Hong said, referring to me.

We ignored him. Soojin pulled up my top lip and examined the area around my missing tooth.

You'll be all right, she said, and I said, Is that the same rifle? From the day we met?

Nope, Soojin said, but didn't go on.

Have you seen Fuji? I said.

Fuji? she said, tilting her head at me. No. Not since the day I dropped you two off. What happened to her?

I don't know, I said.

Soojin grew quiet, pointed back to where we had come from, and said, I heard you did a very bad thing.

I've done a few, I said.

She pulled on my scruff.

They'll be after us, she said. For the medicine. For what you did. For me. It doesn't matter. Now they're on the hunt. You'd think they would have better things to do. After a war.

I asked if they were the people the donkey was talking about.

She said, What in the world, Etna? You're talking to donkeys now?

She had begun to scratch my back with her fingernails. I leaned into the scratching.

Then she got serious and said, They don't want the medicine to go to good people. They use the medicine for themselves or to sell it on the black market.

How do you know who is good? I said.

How do you? Soojin said.

Fuji was good, I said.

Fuji was good, she said.

She turned to Semeru and petted him again.

Hong was keeping guard, pacing. He asked what the plan was. Where the village was. Soojin reached for Hong's wrist, and he stopped pacing.

She said to me: Etna, what are you doing here? It's the Wild West here.

I didn't know what the Wild West was, whether that was different from the West.

I said, Soojin, do you remember the farm?

The farm?

Where you took me from.

She frowned.

You wouldn't have lived, she said, if I didn't take you. The whole coast here? Gone. All the buildings, gone. Animals, gone. The people who made it out. They fled farther south to the refugee camps. I only came back here last year, to find this new chaos. All across the mountains. Yes. Of course, Etna, I remember the farm.

Are we far from it?

She had used her sleeve to wipe away more bloodstains on my mouth and was now running her hand across my coat and examining the bandage and the sides of me, all the bumps and ridges and scars. I let her.

Where are you coming from, Etna? she said. It's not the city. I would've seen you before.

Somewhere else, I said. Farther inland.

How long have you been traveling for?

I have no idea, I said.

And you were with those American soldiers the whole time?

Who else would I be with?

You worked for them?

Yes.

What did you do? Soojin asked.

Land mines, I said. UXOs. IEDs. Road and town clearance, mostly.

Land mines, Soojin repeated. UXOs. IEDs. Jesus, Etna. You know what UXOs and IEDs are, but I bet you don't really know what a piano is.

Get out of my head, I said.

She winked. And then she said, You came all this way to go home?

Yes, I said. I want to go home.

Soojin went quiet again, staring at me.

My darling, she said. There's no home to go back to.

I looked away. I wanted to say that I knew—that all this time I knew, that from the night I decided to leave until now, I had of course always known, but I heard her words and heard them again in my head and nothing changed in me.

I just want to go back, I said.

Why? she said.

I pushed my head against her, hard, and shut my eyes.

To be there, I growled. To see and to smell the place where I was born and used to live. To fall asleep and wake up where I was born and used to live. To remember there was a place before all this where I used to live. To remember there was a place where there were days that passed into other days peacefully, peacefully, without terror, and where other animals I knew and cared about used to live.

Etna, she said, petting me, calming me. You survived. I made you promise to survive, and you did. And you found me.

Take me home, I said, and opened my eyes.

Semeru had been watching us closely as we talked, trying to listen, to follow.

Soojin grabbed my scruff once more, shaking me lightly, and got up. She swung the second medicine bag over her shoulder and brought her rifle to her front. She looked at Semeru and Hong and then at the well.

First the medicine, she said. And then, yes, Etna. I'll take you home.

The village wasn't far. It was set up on a high slope that kept rising over the trees, and as we entered from a path, people came out of their shelters.

For some, I could tell it had been a long time since they had seen dogs. They were either shy or came up to us immediately, gasping or squealing, running their hands over our coats, which Semeru loved.

The humans were in clothes that didn't really fit them, other people's clothes, and some wore shoes or slippers they had made themselves with layers of paper and wood. The shelters they were living in were what remained of the original houses in the village.

I caught the scent of a festering wound. Then an old woman, whom I could smell was losing her memory, sitting on a cane chair outside.

Above us, in the highest house, were two people with binoculars, facing the trees where we had come from. Near them hovered two black dots, then the dots buzzed and flew over us and away.

As we headed here, I had filled Semeru in on how I knew Soojin. It pleased him that we knew each other, so much that he kept saying, We're a pack now. I was glad he had stopped apologizing for not doing anything when the men attacked us.

I could hear a strong river as a child petted us and pulled on our ears.

That's more than a river, Semeru said. He sniffed the air. Do you smell that?

I could. Coffee and rice. The smell flitted past us like a bird through the rain damp that was all around.

Hong got set up in a shelter where there were some people who had survived a house that had collapsed over them. He spent most of the day there, meeting the elderly and the infants, administering medicine.

The second bag he hid away in a shed at the top of the village. And it was there that Semeru and I spent the night on the cool ground drifting in and out of sleep, listening to the village below, to the patterns of footsteps.

I slept. I woke up. Cloud shadows moved over us.

The next time I opened my eyes, it was another afternoon. The last of my bandages were gone—my bite wound had nearly healed; the spot where I had lost a tooth had stopped bleeding—and Soojin was sitting between us on the ground with Semeru's head on her lap.

Beside her was her rifle and a bowl of water collected from the well. Semeru had just taken a drink and had asked her if she ever dreamed of the well.

Soojin leaned down, stroking Semeru's ear, and said that she stopped dreaming when she discovered her gift of being able to communicate with us. Semeru asked when that was, and Soojin said it was when she was a teenager.

I used to live a few hours' walk from here, Soojin said. You would have passed it. It was the village my parents lived in. My mother's name was Faye. She came here after living in a different country because she was sick, actually. She had been working at a factory in a city. She met my father there. My father thought the mountain air here might be good for her. She didn't think she was going to live very long, and she didn't want anything to do with hospitals and doctors. But she lived long enough to have me, if you believe it. And look what I became? The thing she didn't want anything to do with. Isn't it funny how that works? I can say

I want nothing to do with war and maybe my child will start one. So I'm glad I don't have children. Faye didn't live through any of this, thankfully . . .

Though, I don't know, Semeru, she said. My mother was in pain for years. So that's another war, no? But that was a long time ago. If you didn't know, I did what Hong and Emi did during the war. You know Emi, yes? We were, for a time, all at the same field hospital together . . .

And I remember one day a dog was brought in. It was horrible. It was horrible—the dog had been in an ambush with his unit, but I got a chance to talk to her. She was an American dog. A Shepherd mix from New York. Similar to Etna, actually. I've never been to New York, and I never will. She was almost gone, but she just wanted to talk about the valley she was born in. She missed the feel of leaves under her paws. The surprise of spotting a fawn. Lakes scattered about that were like little secrets. That's the last thing she said to me . . .

But now I think maybe it isn't so much a gift, what I can do. Because I think about her. Every time I see a goddamn leaf on the ground here, I think about that American dog and about talking to her. And I don't want to think about her anymore. Do you understand, my darling? I'm getting old. I have only the people in these mountains—some who stay, others who go.

Semeru kept his eyes closed but was listening, his head heavy on her lap. Soojin tilted her head into the sun coming down between the trees.

When I was a child, she said, all I ever wanted was a dog. I was always alone. No siblings. In my own little world, in a village with a stream, I used to imagine I would float down one day to a great adventure. Well, look at me now. I did leave. After I discovered my gift. The gift of being able to talk to you. To the select few. My special ones. And I thought that would be my life. That it was what I was supposed to do. To be with you. And then our world was set on fire. And we fought. We got help from so many other places, and we fought and we pushed back an invasion. And we won. We saved this country. And now look at what we're all doing to each other. You think all of this won't happen again? Of course it will. It always does. We'll rebuild. And then someone—maybe someone from far away, maybe someone who helped rebuild all this—will take a step to burn it down again . . .

I'm just grateful now I have no one to worry about, Soojin said. Is that horrible of me to say? When the next war comes, I won't be around for it. I can sleep every night knowing that. This is how I live now. Inwardly and selfishly, I think, sometimes. This is no place for you two.

Semeru opened his eyes.

But Soojin wasn't speaking to us anymore. She was far away. I thought I heard faint, human singing. She put a hand on Semeru's back and ran her hand down his spine. She did it again. Then she massaged Semeru's ear, and then the other, and she repeated the process over again, from the spine to his ears.

And in his exhaustion, or something else, Semeru began to cry. It sounded like a long, uninterrupted whine, and he grew embarrassed because he couldn't control it, and then it was over. He licked his paws, and she wrapped her arms around him briefly, coming back to us from wherever she had been.

Let me show you what I used to do as a child by the stream, Soojin said.

She gently slipped away from under Semeru and got on her hands and knees. She lifted her nose up to sniff the air and she crawled around and came back so that we were suddenly facing each other. Her tongue stuck out a little. A strand of her hair was stuck on her lip.

Her body was in shadow but her face lit up as she panted like I was panting and touched her nose to mine.

I inhaled rust, a cobweb, rain, and then, faintly, through her open mouth: four tumors deep in her body, possibly another one.

I caught my reflection in her eye. The reflection of her in the reflection of mine.

We'll leave soon, Soojin said. We'll wait for dark and hope they won't follow us in the dark. There's been no activity for a day, so maybe we got lucky. I'll take you home, Etna. As promised. You'll go home the way I'm home . . .

But promise me something, too, Soojin said. You'll take Semeru with you. Promise.

I looked across at Semeru: in that moment, in the way he was lying there, pretending to be asleep, he reminded me of Fuji. And it came to me again how, in her last year with us, she fought as though wanting to go back to the dog she once was. And I wondered if that had still felt possible to her when she left us. If that was why she had left us.

Did that feel possible for me, too?

I turned back to Soojin, who had remained on her hands and knees in front of me.

I promise, I said. I'll take Semeru home with me.

Good, Soojin said, then bumped her nose again to mine.

Wait, I said.

I was about to tell her about the tumors, but she said, I know, Etna. You don't need to tell me. Which means I'll probably never see you two again. So I'm glad I did today and yesterday. We never got to Sicily, Etna. But for two days, I got to have two beautiful dogs.

Soojin stood up. She brushed the dirt off her pants, picked up her rifle, and walked across to join the people at the lookout.

We left at dusk. Hong insisted on coming with us. After they brought Semeru and me to the coast, Soojin would take Hong back to the city.

We walked all night. We walked in the forest under moonlight, and we hardly spoke. Every few minutes, Soojin would turn to check on Hong, who was in the back. He would then check behind us.

I liked seeing the ease between them. Like they had their own language. I liked knowing they had worked together.

It made me think of the dogs I had worked with.

I thought of fawns and leaves under my paws as I walked. And secret lakes. I imagined finding one, somewhere, someday.

(Maybe a well was a secret lake.)

I let Semeru walk a little ahead of me, closer to Soojin. Sometimes he glanced back at me the way Soojin checked on Hong.

Semeru was happy. His brow was soft. He was coming with me.

I was happy, too. He had never been to the coast. Never smelled it. Had never stepped into the sea.

He said, We'll find a good place.

He meant a good place to settle and live, and I said, Yes, we'll find a good place.

I watched as he slipped in and out of the moonlight, and I followed his path, feeling the night on my coat.

I heard the distant gunfire before anyone else did. It was faint, like a wing hitting a branch. I let out a small bark and stopped.

Eyeing me, Soojin lifted her wrist. A small ball the size of a chestnut rose up out of the wide wristband she was wearing and hovered in front of her. Then she pressed a button on the screen attached to the band and the ball flew up and away. I followed the mechanical whir of it for as long as I could.

Hong was standing behind Soojin's shoulder, asking her to switch to the night mode, and the screen lit up green. Semeru and I kept our eyes focused on the way we had come from, ears up and forward, alert.

The range isn't great on this one, Soojin said.

Keep going just a little bit, Hong said.

They were whispering. I heard her finger sliding across the screen.

There, Hong said.

I count five, Soojin said.

Six, Hong said. They must've passed through the village hours ago. They're moving fast.

Soojin cursed. The drone flew back and docked on her wrist. She and Hong checked their rifles, and together we picked up our pace.

Blue began to reappear in the sky, surrounding stars.

We came upon a mountain road. Soojin stepped out first, checking both sides. Up a slope, there was a fork in the road: one that began to descend the mountains and another that went higher.

The higher one had been blocked off with old logs and faded signs with words in many languages and the shapes and symbols I already recognized: WARNING. DO NOT ENTER. UXOs.

Soojin didn't look at me, but I knew what she was thinking.

I said it for her: They wouldn't expect us to go that way.

What are you two talking about? Hong said.

Soojin didn't respond to him. Can you do it? she said to me.

I can do it, I said.

Do what? Semeru said.

I'll need your help, I said to Semeru, who grew lighter on his paws, excited.

Then go do it, Soojin said.

I led Semeru up the road as Hong protested, but halfheartedly, I could tell. I heard Soojin whispering to him as I smelled around the roadblock.

I smelled, then told Semeru that explosives gave off vapors and that we were going to detect them. To search for a smell that was sweet like chewing gum or toothpaste coming up from the dirt. If you smelled it, your job was to stop immediately and let me know. To not move a centimeter until I got there.

I hate toothpaste, Semeru said.

The day began to open up. Hong was keeping an eye on the road; Soojin on us.

I crossed over the logs and the signs and entered the blocked road.

I went first. I told Semeru to follow me every step and to stop when I stopped. I wanted him to double-check my path and make sure it was clear enough for Hong and Soojin to walk along.

I began to sniff. I walked very slowly and carefully with my paws a bit wider and flatter on the ground. I had to smell past the earth and the top layers of earth, past the old blood smell and the skeleton of a bird underground and grass and seeds and,

I thought, rubber, like bits of a tire, past the casing of a bullet, many bullets, wires, minerals.

Chewing gum. Toothpaste. I stopped.

I sat to let Soojin and Hong know I had found one. I stayed to its left and went back where I came, Semeru leading now, and then we started over again, focusing on the left side of the road this time, to widen the path.

That'll take too long, Soojin said. She was already over the logs.

She said always keep to the left of the UXO whenever I detected one and that they would step exactly where I stepped.

We returned to the one I detected and kept going, slowly, across the dirt, nose to the ground.

I was working again. I was suddenly thinking of only this.

I found two more, stopped, sat to show them, and kept to the left, making sure there weren't more on the narrow line of a path I was making for them.

We kept going up the road. The sun rose low on the earth.

Then I found a fourth and was about to step around when Semeru said my name. He was right behind me. He said he thought there was another one right beside my left front paw and that I should check.

I froze. I leaned down, sniffed, and looked back at him.

Well done, I said.

I moved around that one as well, always keeping to the left of the UXOs, our path winding back and forth up the road slowly, slowly, until I couldn't smell them anymore.

I told everyone to wait, and I checked up ahead, the entire width of the road. I went up and down. I then asked Semeru to do the same, and I watched as he followed my path. Hong and Soojin kept checking behind us.

I said that I thought we were clear. Semeru agreed. We were clear.

Good boys, Soojin said, and gave us some of the well water. And then we hurried again, up the road until it went down, the river noise growing louder now, almost taking over all sounds.

It distracted me, the overwhelming noise of the water.

We rounded the curve of the road that hugged the side of the mountain, only to find a part of the mountain had collapsed on top of it.

The road was impassable.

My ears kept filling with the river noise. I dimly heard Soojin cursing. She peered over the edge. We all did now.

I told you that was more than a river, Semeru said.

We were all staring down at the start of a waterfall.

I couldn't see what was beyond it. I couldn't find a way down.

The current was too fast and strong for us to cross to the other side.

I could feel the mist on my whiskers as we retraced our steps and headed back up.

I was watching Soojin and Hong staring at each other, and I could read what was contained in their faces, when a rifle shot cracked through the air so fast that we didn't have time to see where it hit Hong, only that he spun and collapsed.

But Hong was also fast. He dragged himself behind a boulder, where we all hurried and crouched as close to him as possible, behind him, facing the direction of the sound.

I could already smell his blood. And burned skin and metal. Hong was pressing his hand against his wounded shoulder and wincing.

Then he made a joke to me. He said, Look at us and our shoulders.

A voice called out: We just want the dogs!

And that doctor bitch! another shouted.

Hong leaned out from behind the boulder and saw that the last of the men coming for us were making their way across the blocked portion of the road, stepping on top of the footprints and pawprints we had made.

Hong rested his rifle on the boulder and began to fire quickly near the feet of the approaching men on the road.

He shot fast. He hit a mine on the fifth shot, and the mine went off.

The explosion was deafening. The ground erupted. For a moment, there was no air. Only that concussion I had grown too accustomed to. When the sound faded, we heard screaming.

Everyone screamed the same when they got wounded. I learned that. It was impossible to tell one human from another human in these moments.

A cloud of dirt dissipated in the wind.

The top portion of a man was on the ground, his hips and legs entirely severed from his torso. He was trying to hold in his stomach, and he was screaming without pause.

Then there was screaming everywhere, and we ducked behind the boulder and hid from the gunfire that was manic and unending. Soojin blindly fired back.

Hong was bleeding heavily now. The smell was everywhere. I peered around the boulder and saw that one of the men had run away. That plus the dying one meant there were only four now.

Hong said he was going to try to cross over to the tree near the edge to get a better angle.

Soojin kept firing as Hong rushed over and made it to the tree. He faced me and smiled. It was the same big smile as when I met him the first time, when he patched me up by the river.

Then he swung around the tree, lifting his rifle to fire, but the sound I heard wasn't his weapon, it was someone else's, up on the road, and I watched dark mist explode around Hong's head.

For a moment, I thought it was the waterfall flying up. A puff of mist and then Soojin screaming this time as Hong fell backward, over the edge, into the river and down into the waterfall, his body limp and his face frozen in that smile he was giving me.

The shots kept coming. I counted the four hurrying down the mountain road now.

We have to do something, Semeru said.

Before I understood what was happening, Semeru bolted, running up the road again, faster than I had ever seen him go, too fast for the men to aim and fire. He got the left one by the arm and took him down, biting fiercely and quickly, and as the other men aimed at Semeru, I ran up and lunged for the closest one, and Soojin fired at the others. I tore quickly through the man's throat as the fourth man got off a shot, and I looked up to see Semeru stumble as though he had tripped on something.

Soojin fired again, hitting the fourth man in the chest.

I heard another gun go off from someone else, but it was enough time for me to get to Semeru.

The shot had grazed his hind leg. He was hopping, but he could walk, and he said he was fine, and we went back down together.

By then Soojin had also hurried across to the tree.

We just want the dogs! a voice called again. We could use those dogs!

Semeru tried to lick his wound. I counted two now. One of them was bleeding from Semeru attacking him.

I thought they would give up, since there were only two now.

I said, Soojin, look, there's only two, but she didn't respond.

Soojin was barely awake.

She had been hit in the stomach while crossing over to the tree.

Her skin had changed color. I could see the beads of sweat on her forehead and hear the erratic beating of her heart and her cluttered, rough breathing—like the sound of sandpaper on metal.

She opened her eyes. She focused first on the two approaching men, and then behind her at the river and waterfall.

Blood dripped down her chin.

And then, her tongue heavy in her mouth, she said, My beautiful darlings. Follow the water. Forgive me. For it all.

And with whatever energy she had left, she fired another rifle shot at the two men and then wrapped her arms around Semeru, who thought she was hugging him, and Soojin screamed from the pain in her body as she threw Semeru over the edge, into the rushing river.

I saw his pale body flail in the air and water as he went over the waterfall.

I screamed.

I barked.

I kept barking as I felt Soojin's arms around me, too, and then I was up in the air, tall as a human, the world around me tilting and roaring as she threw me into the water.

I flew down.

I went under.

I came up.

I went down.

When I came up again, the water everywhere, inside me, pulling me away fast, I glimpsed Soojin firing at the men one last time, and the men fired back as she tried to jump over the edge, too.

But she fell to her knees by the tree, dropped her rifle, wrapped a hand around her neck, and I went down again.

I couldn't hear. I couldn't smell.

It was almost like sleep.

It was like I wanted to sleep.

I spun and fell. I spun, falling.

I hit rocks. Rocks hit me.

I swallowed water.

Water swallowed me.

I fell, spinning.

I was going so fast. I was pulled and dragged.

Nothing hurt because I was almost asleep.

I thought I was back in the field of the way station, staring at that wall with the pale squares where paintings once hung. A man in a pilot's uniform appeared by the door, and his chest was breaking open like he was sprouting wings, and then I felt a jaw on my scruff as I left the water, was lifted, and was dragged up the bank.

I kept vomiting water. I was both nothing-feeling and everything-feeling. Like the world had poured into me and I was lying on my side, limbs outstretched, trying to push it back out.

I stayed awake long enough to sense the trees around me, so tall, and Semeru looming over me, unclasping his jaw from my body.

I told you, he said. I'm strong.

He coughed. He vomited, too. Then he collapsed on his side, facing me, and we stared at each other as water dripped off his snout, and the noise of the current surrounded us, and his chest rose and fell way too quickly and sped up and shut down, like a door slamming shut, with nothing beating inside him, and I was gone again.

I would never know how long I was there for. How many mornings and nights passed. I lost track. I thought the waking was a dream. I felt neither hunger nor thirst nor my own body. I could smell nothing. It was like I was spinning and falling again. I pawed the space between me and Semeru, thinking I could touch him, and when I couldn't lift my paw anymore, I waited and listened for his heart, for some hint of his voice—for a shape to appear in a space between my eyes.

I kept waiting. And listening.

But there was only the river as I stared at Semeru in the sunlight and moonlight and in rainfall and fog and all over again.

I slept. I woke. Daylight. Moonlight. Fog.

Trees and the moving shadows of trees.

A fly.

It hovered over both of us, buzzing, before it settled on the corner of Semeru's open eye.

I had one dream.

I dreamed Semeru, lying across from me, had a dream about me.

He said the armies had run out of bullets and they had to use dogs to make them. That there were factories that did this. And that he had seen me there, in the factory, waiting to become a bullet.

Could you hear it? Semeru said. Could you hear what they were doing to all of you?

I could smell the terror on him.

They did nothing to me, I said, and woke up.

And then sometime later I heard a creak. The creak of metal. Wheels. A wheelbarrow. Footsteps and a man's heavy breathing as he approached and leaned down, blocking the sun.

I could barely open my eyes. I heard him examining both of us, the ash from his cigarette dropping onto me, and then he picked me up and carried me to the wheelbarrow and laid me down.

I saw myself moving farther away from Semeru, who was still there, so close to the river that if he had awoken, he might've fallen again.

THE SEA

I was born near water.

I can sense the deepness of it even before I open my eyes. I can hear the deep. The far deep. I keep my eyes closed, because it's not unpleasant to keep them closed, and I breathe. I know what I'm smelling, but it's different than I remember.

It's almost like first snow. Sky, the moment it turns to night.

The sun is everywhere. It's all over my snout and ears and the tips of my paws.

I hear a noise that I'm not used to.

I lift my head and try to stand.

I'm weak and shaky. Dizzy. Thirsty. I hurt everywhere.

I try to shake away the hurt and stumble against a bowl of water on the ground.

I drink a little but feel nauseous immediately. I'm drooling.

I take a few steps out from under the tree where I was lying and head toward what I think is a horizon.

But it's a cliff's edge. I want to get closer, but even those few steps are too much, and I collapse. Belly on the grass, I crawl until I can see down below a very long coastline and the beach. Endless blue water.

The tide. That noise: It's the tide. The sound of the breathing tide. Heavy and patient like a hand running through my coat.

In the far distance, to my left, is a point: I can't see what's beyond it. To my right, there's more of the coast; and behind it, inland, there's a mix of forest and broken, burned land that no one has yet built on or touched again.

Lying there near the edge, I keep scanning up and down, looking for something I'll recognize.

How do you feel?

I lift my ears. I try moving my head around, to locate the voice, but I can't tell where it's coming from.

I swivel on the ground without getting up, but I see no one.

I see now a small cottage near the tree I was lying under. I see an open window but no one behind it. Around the side lies a wheelbarrow and a tree stump with an axe. Beside the stump is a watering can and a small turtle's shell standing upright with some pink flowers growing out of it.

Wind pushes some clothes hanging on a line. Listening to the clothes, I stare at the turtle's shell and the swaying tops of the flowers—a word almost comes to me.

Don't worry, the voice says. Achilles will be back. He went down to catch some fish. He's gotten good at it. Clever man. You know, he made the rods himself and wades right in.

My eyes and ears focus up into the tree: an enormous bird is sitting on a branch, staring at me, its wings tucked in.

I don't know what kind of bird it is. I've never seen a bird like her before. She has a thick, sharp beak and her feathers have many colors. Impossible colors.

Her eyes are eyes I've never seen before, either. Like they are breathing, like they carry worlds. I'm shy of them; I fix my gaze at her brightly feathered chest instead.

You said *Achilles,* I say.

I cough. I wince. I try to stand, but I give up and lie back down.

Well, that's the man's name, the bird says.

I'm trying to recall where I've heard that name before. Then, in my mind, floats up a window at night. Semeru beside me.

The Greek? I ask.

The bird cocks her head at me, puzzled.

I mean, he's Greek, the bird says. Yes. He's from Greece. A Greek man. He's the one who found you. You're lucky he did. I might have spotted you, but I would've been too high to notice if you were alive.

I understand now why I couldn't locate her voice: the more she speaks, the more it levels with the tide and they sound like one, like her voice is both coming from her and from a great distance, all around.

But Achilles, the bird says. He goes scavenging sometimes. He brings a wheelbarrow with him. He'll come back with an axe, clothing, shoelaces, a book, phones, though he has no use for those. He just collects the phones and burns them—thinks they should be banished from the earth. No phones in the new world, Achilles says. And no drones.

What kind of bird are you? I say.

The bird blinks, sits up straighter, and puffs up her feathers.

The best kind, she says. An ancient kind. The forever kind. What kind of dog are you?

I try to remember how people described me.

I have no idea, I say.

She grunts in disapproval but doesn't press.

He's harmless, by the way, the bird says. Achilles. People around here have left him alone.

I lift my ears, searching for nearby noises.

Are there many people here? I ask. On the coast?

The bird blinks. Scattered about, yes, she says. And some communities are beginning to form, yes. Everyone is trying to start over again. Of course, there are also people continuing to fight with each other here on the coast, too. Fighting for the usual things. But not as much as in the mountains . . . You know, you could stay with Achilles for a little while if you wanted to. It's comfortable here. It's small but comfortable, and he doesn't get into trouble. He knows how to do things. He's clever.

Clever enough to fish and scavenge, I say.

Good fish, the bird says. Besides, it'd be good for him, too. To have a dog.

Do you stay with him? I ask.

Please, she says loudly, and puffs up her feathers again. No one owns me.

How old are you? I say.

So old I've become young again, she says. It's all a circle, no? We all come back around, don't we?

I don't know, I say. Do we?

Like the tide, the bird says.

I hesitate, trying to understand, but she is speaking in riddles.

A phrase comes back to me: she is *in her own world.*

I am not, she says. I am in this world.

I look at her eyes again but grow shy.

You're the first bird that I've seen, I say. Since I was a pup.

A pup?

Yes, I say, and tell the bird that I have memories of seeing birds around me when I was a puppy, before the war. That I have memories of living with birds.

All these birds, I say. Seabirds, I think. What happened to the birds?

What happened to the dogs? she says back.

I'm not sure how to respond to that. She shifts on the branch, then leans backward and, for a moment, she vanishes into the leaves. Then only her head emerges from the leaves.

Her eyes carry a swirl of sunlight. And the water. And the wind.

I'm still dizzy. I'm imagining all this, I say to myself.

Maybe I'm the one imagining you, the bird says.

I wouldn't mind, I say.

Don't be so hard on yourself, she says. You're here. You're breathing. You arrived and you survived.

A cloud shadow skirts the cliff's edge. I turn again and scan the coast, searching once more for anything familiar. A familiar shape, a noise. I inhale, smelling the sea that is like first snow, like the moment the sky turns to night.

Tell me, I say. Is there a farm nearby? Here?

There were many farms here, the bird says.

I was born on a farm, I say. I think it was around here. Home. I can't smell it from here, but I think I'm close. I have to be close. The wind and the tide. The sand.

And birds, the bird says.

And goats, I say. And a fat pig. And a hornet's nest. Like that turtle's shell over there, but high above me, hanging.

She considers all this, leaning back into the leaves again.

She says, Beyond the point over there. A few hours' walk. I think there was an animal sanctuary. It rescued birds, turtles, goats, all animals. But the soldiers came. I don't need to tell you that. You know. But maybe that's where you were born. If you remember animals.

Yes, I say. All animals. Yes. Maybe. Did a couple live there? A young man and a young woman? They had soft voices.

You have a soft voice, the bird says. Did you know that?

I had never considered my voice. I shut my eyes and see my mother stepping over me like a giant. The triangle of her ears like sails.

Were they kind? I say.

Who?

The humans who worked on the farm. Were they kind?

Does it matter? the bird asks.

Yes, I say. I think it does. To me. Yes.

They were kind, the bird says. They stayed until the end. They didn't abandon the animals.

Good, I say. That's good.

The dizziness has begun to go away, but I still feel the hurt all over, heavy inside me. I force myself to stretch out. I hear my body rubbing across the grass. A breeze comes in again, over me, pushing the clothes on the line.

Now I can see the man who must be Achilles appearing from out of the forest below. He's carrying his fishing rods, and he has a beard, and he's shirtless. He's tan, with a wide chest, and his pants are rolled up to his shins. His hair is long and wrapped up in a bun.

When did he get here? I say. Achilles.

Near the end, the bird says. He came out of the forest, found this abandoned house, moved in, and he never went back to where he came from. Now look at him. Tell me, what is your name?

When the bird says this, I hesitate. I try to remember what the farm owners used to call me. I have not thought about that in years. A shape forms on my tongue but vanishes.

Etna, I say. My name is Etna.

Etna, the bird repeats. Etna. Like the volcano. In Sicily.

Have you ever seen a volcano? I ask.

You mean, when it erupts? the bird says. Sure I have.

What's it like? I ask.

What's it like? It's like what your name means, I think, in Greek.

And what does my name mean in Greek?

You don't know?

No.

To burn, the bird says. It means, *To burn.*

To burn, I repeat.

Yes.

Maybe one day I'll go to Sicily, I say. Or Greece.

The bird says, Close your eyes. Now open them. Voila. You're in Sicily. Or Greece. You couldn't tell the difference.

She's trying to make me smile. I'm watching Achilles below, lifting his arm and spearing rods into the sand.

When I don't smile, the bird says: Would you like me to see what's left of the farm?

I tell her yes.

Then I add: but after the waterfall. Could you go to the waterfall first? There's a dog. On the banks. Could you check if he's still there? His name is Semeru. And there's a man. His name is Hong. I think he's somewhere near the bottom of the waterfall, too.

Were they your friends? the bird says.

Yes, I say. They were my friends. They were . . .

They were your pack, she says. And they came with you.

They came all the way, I say.

The bird blinks and ruffles her feathers again.

They came *for* you, she says. They came and they died. And you don't know how to feel about that. Or you're feeling many things right now. All these things that humans love to write poems about. Have you ever listened to a poem? That's how humans really sing, isn't it? But these feelings you're feeling, Etna, are also feelings from not just what happened now, but from the years. These miserable years.

Listening to her, I shut my eyes.

We need friends, Etna, the bird says. We need a pack.

Even if we lose our pack, I say.

Especially because of that, she says.

Then she adds: Don't be alone like me, Etna.

I open my eyes.

Are you alone? I ask.

She goes silent. I listen to the tide and the leaves in the trees and then she says, I'll go find them. I promise. And I'll go see about the farm.

But she doesn't leave, not yet. She shifts on the branch again with her large claws, a leaf falls, and she points her beak at me and says, You've traveled far.

Flashes of landscapes flicker across my mind.

She asks for how long I've been traveling, but I don't know, I've lost track. Nights and nights and nights.

I see moonlight and thin trees. A helmet filled with old rain. The old dog. A skeleton inside an airplane.

She says, What now? What's next?

I cup the wind in my ears, following Achilles, and then move across to the distant point that hides whatever lies behind it.

I had wanted to come here. I left and I traveled far. I fought after the fighting was over. I kept moving. I survived.

I made it home, I think. I'm here.

But I'm not sure what to do now, now that I'm here. I'm not sure what to do. I'm here, and yet nothing familiar has come to me, as though I'm still far away, still moving. Like I haven't yet arrived. Or like I've come here for the first time, smelling and seeing things here for the first time. Everything new and unknown.

Do you dream? I ask the bird.

Of course I dream, she says.

What do you dream about?

The bird thinks about how to answer this.

Finally she says, Being unable to find somewhere to land. I dream about being unable to find somewhere to land. I'm high in the air and peer down and there is nothing. Not even water. I mean, literally. There is nothing. I'm the last thing left.

In the world?

In the entire world.

What did you do? I say. During the war. How did you survive?

Which war? she says.

Which war, I think.

I lick my paws and taste the remnants of the waterfall. Soojin's blood. With the tip of my tongue, I press a speck of Soojin's blood into the space where I once had a tooth.

I inhale deeply. I breathe. I feel her blood enter me the way snowflakes melt into me.

The bird watches.

Etna, she says. May I listen to your heart?

Slowly, I roll over onto my side on the grass. The grass bends and glides over my snout.

I let her listen to my heart.

She hums, almost a song.

After a moment she says, Would you like to know?

Why not, I say, which makes her hoot like an owl. The sound is like a fluttering inside her that leaps over and along my spine.

Don't worry, she says. You still have a long time, Etna.

The wind blows again, stronger this time. Achilles sticks the last rod into the sand and stands there, staring out at the water, the wind moving through his beard.

My coat has dried. I listen to my own breathing. I think of Semeru, and I think of the way station, and I think of the doctor, whose name I can't remember, who is lying on her side alone, waiting forever in the city at the clinic for Hong, the way Jason and Brian are forever on the floor of a valley.

I think of an empty bird's nest, and I think of a slow-moving train in the mountains and a letter in a shirt pocket.

I think the pink flowers in the turtle's shell behind me are called azaleas.

I ask the bird if she's ever seen a dog named Fuji on the coast with blue eyes, a pale stripe on her chest, and a mole on her tongue.

She was also my friend, I say. She was also my pack.

The bird blinks, considering my words.

I'm sorry, she says. I haven't seen her. Not on this coast, not anywhere. But look! Over there, Etna. Look! See the dogs.

I lift my head; I look. Near the point, I spot three dogs trotting along the beach. Even from here, I can tell by their limbs that they are very young. And healthier than I am. One begins to play in the water, and another follows.

Who are they? I ask.

They seem impossibly far, and heading farther toward the point.

Your future, the bird says.

And then she says, You'll find them when the time comes. Or they'll find you. And you'll tell each other your stories. You'll take care of one another. You'll be a good pack. They're good dogs, and you'll start anew with them; and with them, you'll get to know this place again, Etna. Now let me go check on the things you want me to check on.

I keep watching the dogs in the distance. I hear their paws in the tide. A fish being caught on a line.

I say, Bird, what's your name? What are you called?

But I hear wings. Her wings. I feel them inside me. Deep in my chest. Against the curve of my ribs. Their tremendous movements. Their bright sound and their infinite span.

The air around me quakes. Her flight takes my breath away.

She's gone.

I don't see her anymore. I don't hear her anymore.

I hear the sea. And the sand floating in the wind. And the wind over the grass. I hear nothing else but the sea and the sand in the wind and the trembling grass.

The young dogs, too, are gone.

I breathe. I stand up carefully in the wind and the sun.

This time I stay standing. I lean out once toward all the blue, and then I walk to the shade of the tree to rest, to recover, and to wait.

AUTHOR'S NOTE

This book was inspired by the novel, *King*, which was written by John Berger, whose work I began reading over twenty years ago. Though I never got a chance to meet him, I remain forever indebted to him, and forever indebted to the grace and humanity of his art.

The Louise Glück excerpt is taken from her poem "March," in *A Village Life* (FSG).

The J. M. Ledgard line is from his novel *Giraffe* (The Penguin Press).

Thank you to my pack: Marion, Simon, M.C., Rebecca, the Clegg Agency, Jon, Stu, Emma, Kayley, Stacey, Jaime, John Mark, Colleen, Scribner, S&S, Anna & WME, Oliver, Left Bank Ciders & my Northern Spies, Hudson/Catskill, Don, Ethan, Caroline, Katie, Ralph & Gwen, Bread Loaf, Elliott & Lauren, Laura, and all the dogs.